序

　　承辦全民英檢的「語言訓練測驗中心」，在網站上公佈了「全民英檢參考字表」，初級有 2263 個字。根據他們的說法，初級檢定的試題中，約有百分之九十，出自他們所公佈的字彙。

　　「初級英檢公佈字彙」多於「大考中心」所公佈的「國中、小學兩千字表」，增加了一些較難的單字，如 achieve、admit、adopt、affair、AIDS、aircraft、apply 等，這些都是考試中常考的。我們又審慎挑選一些常考的單字，如 ease、earrings、dodge ball 等，希望字彙命中率能達到百分之九十五以上。

　　碰到不會的單字，可用「比較法」來背，例如：cross（橫越）你不會，但你認識 across 這個介系詞，兩個字一比較，兩個字都認識了，而且記得牢。

有些字看起來長，其實很簡單，只要把那個字的字尾去掉就很好背，如 addition（添加；加法），把字尾的 ition 去掉，只要背 add 就行了。長的單字要分音節來背，人類短暫記憶是有限的，例如：23895212 這個數字不好背，但是如果分開來 2-389-5212 就容易多了。單字一定要唸出來，否則很快就會忘記。

　　背英文單字，千萬不要死背，死背會忘記。背第一遍的時候，先把不會的單字做個記號，第二次還不會，再做一次記號，以此類推，複習時，從自己最不會的單字開始，就可以節省很多時間。

　　背英文單字是一項最好的投資。愈背，你的記憶力會愈好，讀者可以和同學比賽，看誰先背好，說不定你會嚇一跳，你的記憶力是如此地驚人！年紀愈小，記憶力愈好。

　　　　　　　　　　　編者　謹識

A a

a 〔ə,e〕 *art.* 一個

Mary has *a* brother and *a* sister.

A.M. 〔'e'ɛm〕 *adv.* 上午 (= *a.m.* = *AM*)

I will meet you at 8:15 *A.M.*

ability 〔ə'bɪlətɪ〕 *n.* 能力

He has unusual *ability* in English.

able 〔'ebḷ〕 *adj.* 能…的

Nick is not *able* to come to the party.

about 〔ə'baʊt〕 *prep.* 關於

This book is *about* cars.

above 〔ə'bʌv〕 *prep.* 在…上面

The kite is flying *above* the tree.

abroad 〔ə'brɔd〕 *adv.* 到國外

Have you ever traveled *abroad*?

absent 〔'æbsṇt〕 *adj.* 缺席的

Bill is *absent* from school today.

accept 〔 ək'sɛpt 〕 *v.* 接受

I *accept* your gift.

accident 〔'æksədənt 〕 *n.* 意外

He was killed in a traffic *accident*.

achieve 〔 ə'tʃiv 〕 *v.* 達到

He worked hard to *achieve* his purpose.

across 〔 ə'krɔs 〕 *prep.* 橫越

Look! There is a dog running *across* the road!

act 〔 ækt 〕 *v.* 行為

He *acted* foolishly.

action 〔'ækʃən 〕 *n.* 行動

Actions speak louder than words.

active 〔'æktɪv 〕 *adj.* 活躍的

Although he is over 80, he's still very *active*.

activity 〔 æk'tɪvətɪ〕 *n.* 活動

Mary is involved in a lot of school *activities*.

actor 〔'æktɚ 〕 *n.* 男演員

Tom Cruise is a famous film *actor*.

actress (ˈæktrɪs) *n.* 女演員

Sarah wants to be an *actress*.

actually (ˈæktʃʊəlɪ) *adv.* 實際上

She looked old, but *actually* she was very young.

add (æd) *v.* 增加

The fire is going out; will you *add* some wood?

addition (əˈdɪʃən) *n.* 添加物；加法

There is no room for *additions*.

address (əˈdrɛs, ˈædrɛs) *n.* 住址

Sue's *address* is written on the envelope.

admire (ədˈmaɪr) *v.* 欽佩

We *admire* her for her honesty.

admit (ədˈmɪt) *v.* 承認

He *admitted* having stolen the money.

adopt (əˈdɑpt) *v.* 採用

I like your methods of teaching and I shall *adopt* them in my school.

adult 〔 ə'dʌlt 〕 *n.* 成人
An *adult* has more responsibility than a child.

advance 〔 əd'væns 〕 *v.* 前進
The troops *advanced*.

advantage 〔 əd'væntɪdʒ 〕 *n.* 優點
He has the *advantage* of good health.

advertisement 〔 ˌædvə'taɪzmənt 〕 *n.* 廣告
Advertisement helps to sell goods.

advice 〔 əd'vaɪs 〕 *n.* 忠告
He wanted my *advice* on the matter.

advise 〔 əd'vaɪz 〕 *v.* 勸告
There is no one to *advise* me.

a few *adj.* 一些
There are *a few* books on the table.

affair 〔 ə'fɛr 〕 *n.* 事情
He has many *affairs* to look after.

affect 〔 ə'fɛkt 〕 *v.* 影響
Smoking *affected* his health.

afraid (ə'fred) *adj.* 害怕的
Don't be *afraid* of my puppy.

after ('æftə) *prep.* 在⋯之後
Monday comes *after* Sunday.

afternoon (ˌæftə'nun) *n.* 下午
My father jogs every *afternoon*.

again (ə'gɛn) *adv.* 再一次
Jim has read that book, but he is reading it *again*.

against (ə'gɛnst) *prep.* 反對；對抗
Are you for or *against* it?

age (edʒ) *n.* 年齡
What's the *age* of that old building?

ago (ə'go) *adv.* ⋯以前
I went to France about two years *ago*.

agree (ə'gri) *v.* 同意
We all *agree* with you.

ahead (ə'hɛd) *adv.* 在前面
John ran *ahead* of the other boys.

aid 〔 ed 〕 *n.* 幫助

He deserves our *aid*.

AIDS 〔 edz 〕 *n.* 愛滋病

AIDS means Acquired Immune Deficiency Syndrome.

aim 〔 em 〕 *n.* 目標

My *aim* is to become an English teacher.

air 〔 ɛr 〕 *n.* 空氣

I need some fresh *air*.

air conditioner *n.* 冷氣機

We need a new *air conditioner*.

aircraft 〔'ɛr,kræft 〕 *n.* 飛機

There are three *aircraft* on the runway.

airlines 〔'ɛr,laɪnz 〕 *n.* 航空公司

I often travel by China *Airlines*.

airplane 〔'ɛr,plen 〕 *n.* 飛機 (= *plane*)

He took a trip by *airplane*.

airport 〔'ɛr,port 〕 *n.* 機場

An *airport* is a busy place.

alarm 〔 ə'lɑrm 〕 *v.* 使驚慌
She was *alarmed* at the sight of the stranger.

album 〔 'ælbəm 〕 *n.* 相簿
I have two photo *albums*.

alike 〔 ə'laɪk 〕 *adj.* 相像的
Their opinions are much *alike*.

a little   *adj.* 一些
There is *a little* milk in the glass.

alive 〔 ə'laɪv 〕 *adj.* 活的
In the burning building, one man was dead but six were still *alive*.

all 〔 ɔl 〕 *adj.* 全部的
Sally read *all* the books.

allow 〔 ə'laʊ 〕 *v.* 允許
The teacher *allowed* John to leave the classroom.

almost 〔 'ɔl,most 〕 *adv.* 幾乎
Dinner is *almost* ready.

alone 〔 ə'lon 〕 *adj.* 單獨的
Parents should never leave children *alone*
at night.

along 〔 ə'lɔŋ 〕 *prep.* 沿著
She walked *along* the street with her mother.

a lot *adv.* 很多
You've changed *a lot*.

aloud 〔 ə'laʊd 〕 *adv.* 出聲地；大聲地
The teacher asked me to read the poem *aloud*.
The hungry baby cried *aloud*.

alphabet 〔'ælfə,bɛt 〕 *n.* 字母（表）
A, B, and C are the first three letters of the
English *alphabet*.

already 〔 ɔl'rɛdɪ 〕 *adv.* 已經
She has *already* finished her homework.

also 〔'ɔlso 〕 *adv.* 也
He is kind and *also* honest.

although 〔 ɔl'ðo 〕 *conj.* 雖然
Although it was raining, Joan still wanted
to go out.

altogether 〔ˌɔltə'gɛðə〕 *adv.* 總共
There are seven of us *altogether*.

always 〔'ɔlwez〕 *adv.* 總是
The bus *always* comes at seven.

am 〔æm〕 *v.* be 的第一人稱
I *am* an outgoing person.

ambulance 〔'æmbjələns〕 *n.* 救護車
We saw an *ambulance* rushing to the hospital.

America 〔ə'mɛrɪkə〕 *n.* 美國 (= *the U.S.A.*)
She moved to *America* two years ago.

American 〔ə'mɛrɪkən〕 *n.* 美國人
There are two *Americans* in her class.

among 〔ə'mʌŋ〕 *prep.* 在…之中
She was sitting *among* the boys.

amount 〔ə'maʊnt〕 *n.* 數量
He paid a large *amount* of money.

an 〔æn〕 *art.* 一個
Which is bigger, *an* orange or *an* egg?

ancient〔'enʃənt〕*adj.* 古老的

There are some *ancient* weapons in the museum.

and〔ɛnd〕*conj.* 和

The children sang *and* danced at the party.

angel〔'endʒəl〕*n.* 天使

In pictures *angels* are usually dressed in white and have wings.

anger〔'æŋgɚ〕*n.* 憤怒

The two boys were full of *anger*.

angry〔'æŋgrɪ〕*adj.* 生氣的

Mother was *angry* when John cried.

animal〔'ænəml̩〕*n.* 動物

There are many *animals* in the zoo.

ankle〔'æŋkl̩〕*n.* 腳踝

Sam hurt his *ankle*.

another〔ə'nʌðɚ〕*adj.* 另一個

The shirt is too small; I need *another* one.

answer ('ænsɚ) v. 回答

The question is so difficult that we can't *answer* it.

ant (ænt) n. 螞蟻

An *ant* is a small insect.

any ('ɛnɪ) adj. 任何的

There isn't *any* sugar in the jar.

anybody ('ɛnɪ,badɪ) pron. 任何人 (= *anyone*)

Did he leave a message for *anybody*?

anyone ('ɛnɪ,wʌn) pron. 任何人 (= *anybody*)

If *anyone* calls, tell him I'll be back at five.

anything ('ɛnɪ,θɪŋ) pron. 任何東西

Is there *anything* in your bag?

anyway ('ɛnɪ,we) adv. 不管怎樣；無論如何

Anyway, it's not fair.

anywhere ('ɛnɪ,hwɛr) adv. 任何地方
(= *anyplace*)

Lisa has never been *anywhere* outside her country.

apartment 〔 ə'pɑrtmənt 〕 *n.* 公寓
(= *flat* 〔 flæt 〕【英式用法】)
Ben and his sister lived in an *apartment*.

apologize 〔 ə'pɑlə,dʒaɪz 〕 *v.* 道歉
(= *apologise*【英式用法】)
He *apologized* to her for not going to her party.

appear 〔 ə'pɪr 〕 *v.* 出現
A rainbow always *appears* after the rain.

appearance 〔 ə'pɪrəns 〕 *n.* 外表
Don't judge by *appearances*.

apple 〔'æpḷ 〕 *n.* 蘋果
An *apple* a day keeps the doctor away.

apply 〔 ə'plaɪ 〕 *v.* 申請
I want to *apply* for the scholarship.

appreciate 〔 ə'priʃɪ,et 〕 *v.* 感激
I greatly *appreciate* your kindness.

April 〔'eprəl 〕 *n.* 四月 (= *Apr.*)
April is the fourth month of the year.

are ﹝ɑr﹞ v. be 的第二人稱與各人稱的複數
Cindy and Lucy *are* good friends.

area ﹝'ɛrɪə﹞ n. 地區
Does she live in this *area*?

argue ﹝'ɑrgjʊ﹞ v. 爭論
I'm not going to *argue* with you tonight.

arm ﹝ɑrm﹞ n. 手臂
He fell down and hurt his left *arm*.

armchair ﹝'ɑrm,tʃɛr﹞ n. 扶手椅
The woman is resting in the *armchair*.

army ﹝'ɑrmɪ﹞ n. 軍隊
There they formed an *army* of about two
thousand men.

around ﹝ə'raʊnd﹞ prep. 環繞
He walked *around* the park three times.

arrange ﹝ə'rendʒ﹞ v. 安排
The meeting has been *arranged* for tonight.

arrest ﹝ə'rɛst﹞ v. 逮捕
He was *arrested* for theft.

arrive ﹝ə'raɪv﹞ *v.* 到達
The Dalai Lama will *arrive* here on Monday.

art ﹝ɑrt﹞ *n.* 藝術
Drawing pictures is an *art*.

article ﹝'ɑrtɪkḷ﹞ *n.* 文章
He contributed *articles* to the Central Daily
News frequently.

artist ﹝'ɑrtɪst﹞ *n.* 藝術家
Mary is talking with an *artist*.

as ﹝æz﹞ *prep.* 作為
It can be used *as* a knife.

Asia ﹝'eʃə﹞ *n.* 亞洲
Some of the world's highest mountains are in
Asia.

Asian ﹝'eʃən﹞ *adj.* 亞洲的
Japan, Korea, and India are all *Asian*
countries.

ask ﹝æsk﹞ *v.* 問
She *asked* me how to get there.

asleep ﹝ ə'slip ﹞ *adj.* 睡著的
Sally was so tired that she fell *asleep* right away.

assistant ﹝ ə'sɪstənt ﹞ *n.* 助手
She is my *assistant*.

assume ﹝ ə'sjum ﹞ *v.* 認為
I *assumed* that he had taken the medicine.

at ﹝ æt ﹞ *prep.* 在⋯
There is someone *at* the door.

attack ﹝ ə'tæk ﹞ *v.* 攻擊
The tiger *attacked* and killed a deer for food.

attend ﹝ ə'tɛnd ﹞ *v.* 上（學）；參加
He *attends* school regularly.

attention ﹝ ə'tɛnʃən ﹞ *n.* 注意
Pay *attention* to what I say in class.

audience ﹝ 'ɔdɪəns ﹞ *n.* 觀眾
There was a small *audience*.

August 〔'ɔgəst 〕 *n.* 八月 (= *Aug.*)
August is the eighth month of the year.

aunt 〔 ænt 〕 *n.* 阿姨 (= *auntie* = *aunty*)
My *aunt* is coming to see us.

Australia 〔 ɔ'streljə 〕 *n.* 澳洲
I've never been to *Australia*.

Australian 〔 ɔ'streljən 〕 *adj.* 澳洲的
The koala is an *Australian* animal.

autumn 〔'ɔtəm 〕 *n.* 秋天 (= *fall*)
Autumn is the season between summer and winter.

available 〔 ə'veləbḷ 〕 *adj.* 可獲得的
The book was not *available* in Japan.

avoid 〔 ə'vɔɪd 〕 *v.* 避免
Women should *avoid* driving alone at night.

aware 〔 ə'wɛr 〕 *adj.* 知道的;察覺到的
He was *aware* of the danger.

away (ə'we) *adv.* 離去
They're *away* on holiday.

B b

baby ('bebɪ) *n.* 嬰兒
Both the mother and the *baby* are doing well.

baby-sitter ('bebɪ,sɪtɚ) *n.* 臨時保姆
Lucy's part-time job is being a *baby-sitter*.

back (bæk) *n.* 背面
The price is on the *back* of the book.

backward ('bækwɚd) *adv.* 向後
(= *backwards* 【英式用法】)
She looked *backward* over her shoulder.

bad (bæd) *adj.* 不好的
The weather was really *bad*.

badminton ('bædmɪntən) *n.* 羽毛球
Badminton is a very interesting sport.

bag (bæg) *n.* 袋子
Tom carried a *bag* to school.

bake〔bek〕*v.* 烘烤
I like to *bake* cakes from time to time.

bakery〔'bekərı〕*n.* 麵包店
There is a very good *bakery* near my house.

balcony〔'bælkənı〕*n.* 陽台
You can see the ocean from our *balcony*.

ball〔bɔl〕*n.* 球
We need a *ball* to play basketball.

balloon〔bə'lun〕*n.* 氣球
They blew up *balloons* for the party.

banana〔bə'nænə〕*n.* 香蕉
Monkeys like to eat *bananas*.

band〔bænd〕*n.* 樂隊
The *band* is playing.

bank〔bæŋk〕*n.* 銀行
Albert puts his money in the *bank*.

banker〔'bæŋkɚ〕*n.* 銀行家;銀行業者
Her father is a *banker*.

bar (bɑr) *n.* 酒吧
He went to that *bar* yesterday.

barbecue ('bɑrbɪ,kju) *n.* 烤肉 (= *Bar-B-Q*)
We'll have a *barbecue* this Friday.

barber ('bɑrbɚ) *n.* 理髮師
My uncle is a *barber*.

bark (bɑrk) *v.* 吠叫
What are the dogs *barking* at?

base (bes) *n.* 基礎
He used Stephen King's novel as the *base*
of his movie.

baseball ('bes'bɔl) *n.* 棒球
Baseball is very popular in America.

basement ('besmənt) *n.* 地下室
A house with a *basement* is for sale.

basic ('besɪk) *adj.* 基本的
The *basic* stories of fairy tales never
change.

basis ('besɪs) *n.* 基礎

The farmers form the *basis* of a nation.

basket ('bæskɪt) *n.* 籃子

This *basket* is made of bamboo.

basketball ('bæskɪt,bɔl) *n.* 籃球

We play *basketball* every day.

bat (bæt) *n.* 球棒

Ben used a *bat* to hit the ball in the game.

bath (bæθ) *n.* 洗澡

Sue took a *bath* because she was dirty.

bathe (beð) *v.* 給…洗澡

Will you help me *bathe* the baby?

bathroom ('bæθ,rum) *n.* 浴室

She went into the *bathroom* and took a shower.

be (bi) *v.* 是；成為

I want to *be* a teacher.

beach (bitʃ) *n.* 海灘

John likes to go to the *beach*.

bean (bin) *n.* 豆子
A *bean* is a vegetable.

bear (bɛr) *n.* 熊　　*v.* 忍受
A *bear* is a wild animal.
I can't *bear* the noise anymore.

beard (bɪrd) *n.* 鬍子
My uncle has a long black *beard*.

beat (bit) *v.* 打
He *beat* the drum with a stick.

beautiful ('bjutəfəl) *adj.* 美麗的
The flowers in the garden look so *beautiful*.

beauty ('bjutɪ) *n.* 美麗
Her *beauty* is beyond description.

because (bɪ'kɔz) *conj.* 因為
Linda was late *because* it was raining.

become (bɪ'kʌm) *v.* 變成
They *became* good friends at once.

bed (bɛd) *n.* 床
I fell off my *bed* last night.

bedroom 〔'bɛd,rum 〕 *n.* 臥室

I have my own *bedroom*.

bee 〔 bi 〕 *n.* 蜜蜂

A *bee* is an insect which makes honey.

beef 〔 bif 〕 *n.* 牛肉

You can buy *beef* from a butcher.

been 〔 bin 〕 *v.* be 的過去分詞

He has *been* a teacher since 1990.

beer 〔 bɪr 〕 *n.* 啤酒

Buy me a *beer*, Jack.

before 〔 bɪ'for 〕 *conj.* 在…之前

You must wash your hands *before* you eat.

begin 〔 bɪ'gɪn 〕 *v.* 開始

School *begins* at eight in the morning.

beginner 〔 bɪ'gɪnɚ 〕 *n.* 初學者

He drives better than most *beginners*.

beginning 〔 bɪ'gɪnɪŋ 〕 *n.* 開始

I missed the *beginning* of the film.

behave ﹝ bɪ'hev ﹞ *v.* 行為舉止
Jim always *behaves* well.

behind ﹝ bɪ'haɪnd ﹞ *prep.* 在…後面
The playground is *behind* our school.

belief ﹝ bɪ'lif ﹞ *n.* 相信;信仰
She was beautiful beyond *belief*.

believe ﹝ bɪ'liv ﹞ *v.* 相信
Do you *believe* in magic?

bell ﹝ bɛl ﹞ *n.* 鐘;鈴
I can hear the church *bell* ringing.

belong ﹝ bə'lɔŋ ﹞ *v.* 屬於
This book *belongs* to me.

below ﹝ bə'lo ﹞ *prep.* 在…以下
Students who have marks *below* 60 will have
to take the exam again.

belt ﹝ bɛlt ﹞ *n.* 皮帶
Rose gave a *belt* to her father on his
birthday.

bench ﹝ bɛntʃ ﹞ *n.* 長椅

The man has been sitting on the *bench* all day long.

beside ﹝ bɪˈsaɪd ﹞ *prep.* 在…旁邊

Pat and Paul sat *beside* each other in class.

besides ﹝ bɪˈsaɪdz ﹞ *adv.* 此外

It's too late to go out now. *Besides*, it's beginning to rain.

best ﹝ bɛst ﹞ *adj.* 最好的

It is *best* to start it now.

better ﹝ ˈbɛtɚ ﹞ *adj.* 較好的

It's *better* than nothing.

between ﹝ bəˈtwin ﹞ *prep.* 在（兩者）之間

The boy is standing *between* two trees.

beyond ﹝ bɪˈjɑnd ﹞ *prep.* 超過

Many people don't go on working *beyond* the age of 65.

bicycle ﹝ ˈbaɪsɪkḷ ﹞ *n.* 腳踏車（ = *bike*)

Do you know who stole the *bicycle*?

big 〔 bɪg 〕 *adj.* 大的

An elephant is a *big* animal.

bike 〔 baɪk 〕 *n.* 腳踏車

He goes to school by *bike*.

bill 〔 bɪl 〕 *n.* 帳單

The man is looking at the *bill*.

biology 〔 baɪˈɑlədʒɪ 〕 *n.* 生物學

Biology is my favorite subject.

bird 〔 bɝd 〕 *n.* 鳥

Most *birds* can fly.

birthday 〔 ˈbɝθ,de 〕 *n.* 生日

For her *birthday* I bought her a doll.

bit 〔 bɪt 〕 *n.* 一點；少許

We need only a *bit*.

bite 〔 baɪt 〕 *v.* 咬

Don't let the puppy *bite* your hand.

bitter 〔 ˈbɪtɚ 〕 *adj.* 苦的

The medicine tastes *bitter*.

black 〔 blæk 〕 *adj.* 黑的
Sue's hair is *black*.

blackboard 〔'blæk‚bord 〕 *n.* 黑板
The teacher writes a sentence on the
blackboard.

blame 〔 blem 〕 *v.* 責備
He *blamed* you for being late.

blank 〔 blæŋk 〕 *adj.* 空白的
He handed in a *blank* piece of paper.

blanket 〔'blæŋkɪt 〕 *n.* 毯子
The baby is covered with the *blanket*.

blind 〔 blaɪnd 〕 *adj.* 盲的
Blind children have to go to special schools.

block 〔 blɑk 〕 *n.* 街區
The store is three *blocks* away.

blood 〔 blʌd 〕 *n.* 血
A lot of people are afraid of *blood*.

blouse 〔 blaʊz 〕 *n.* 女用上衣
Wendy wears a white *blouse* to school.

blow〔 blo 〕*v.* 吹

She *blows* her hair dry.

blue 〔 blu 〕*adj.* 藍色的

Helen is wearing a *blue* dress.

board 〔 bord 〕*n.* 木板   *v.* 上（車、船、飛機）

The floor was partly of *boards* and partly of stone.

The passengers *boarded* the plane at the airport in London.

boat 〔 bot 〕*n.* 船

Tom and Dan are on a *boat*.

body 〔'badɪ 〕*n.* 身體

Eat right and you will have a healthy *body*.

boil 〔 bɔɪl 〕*v.* 沸騰

The water is *boiling*.

bomb 〔 bɑm 〕*n.* 炸彈

A *bomb* exploded and destroyed many houses.

bone 〔 bon 〕*n.* 骨頭

An old woman doesn't have strong *bones*.

book 〔 bʊk 〕 *n.* 書　 *v.* 預訂

Anna read a lot of *books* before the exam.

I'll call them to *book* a room.

bookcase 〔'bʊkˌkes 〕 *n.* 書架

Can you put the *bookcase* over there?

bookstore 〔'bʊkˌstor 〕 *n.* 書店

Tom is going to the *bookstore* to buy a book.

bored 〔 bord 〕 *adj.* 感到無聊的

The students were *bored* with the lesson.

boring 〔'borɪŋ 〕 *adj.* 無聊的

Martin feels that typing is a *boring* job.

born 〔 bɔrn 〕 *adj.* 出生的

The kitten was *born* yesterday.

borrow 〔'baro 〕 *v.* 借（入）

May I *borrow* your bicycle for a day?

boss 〔 bɔs 〕 *n.* 老闆

The new *boss* is very strict.

both 〔 boθ 〕 *pron.* 兩者都

Sharon and Mark *both* came to class late.

bother 〔'baðæ〕 v. 打擾

Don't *bother* Tina with that now — she is busy.

bottle 〔'batḷ〕 n. 瓶子

Harry is pouring a drink from a *bottle*.

bottom 〔'batəm〕 n. 底部

The ship sank to the *bottom* of the sea.

bow 〔baʊ〕 v. 鞠躬

The student *bowed* to his teacher.

bowl 〔bol〕 n. 碗

He has finished five *bowls* of rice.

bowling 〔'bolɪŋ〕 n. 打保齡球

Jeff goes *bowling* every week.

box 〔baks〕 n. 盒子

Linda gave me a *box* of candies.

boy 〔bɔɪ〕 n. 男孩

Billy is a naughty *boy* who lives near my house.

brain 〔bren〕 n. 頭腦

She has a good *brain* and beauty.

branch〔bræntʃ〕*n.* 樹枝

A bird is sitting on a *branch* in my garden.

brave〔brev〕*adj.* 勇敢的

Firemen are *brave* people.

bread〔brɛd〕*n.* 麵包

Bread is made from flour.

break〔brek〕*v.* 打破

Who *broke* the window?

breakfast〔ˈbrɛkfəst〕*n.* 早餐

We always have *breakfast* at 7:00 a.m.

brick〔brɪk〕*n.* 磚頭

The house is made of red *brick*.

bridge〔brɪdʒ〕*n.* 橋

There is a *bridge* across the river.

brief〔brif〕*adj.* 簡短的

He gave a *brief* talk to the students.

bright〔braɪt〕*adj.* 明亮的

The box was painted *bright* green.

bring〔brɪŋ〕v. 帶來
I *brought* the book you wanted.

Britain〔'brɪtən〕n. 英國
Jim went to *Britain* last summer.

British〔'brɪtɪʃ〕adj. 英國的
He planned to visit his *British* friends.

broad〔brɔd〕adj. 寬廣的
This is a *broad* street.

broadcast〔'brɔd͵kæst〕v. 廣播;播出
The TV station *broadcasts* the show every day.

brother〔'brʌðɚ〕n. 兄弟
These two boys are *brothers*.

brown〔braʊn〕adj. 棕色的
John likes to wear *brown* shoes.

brunch〔brʌntʃ〕n. 早午餐
We are used to eating *brunch* on weekends.

brush〔brʌʃ〕n. 刷子
William uses a small *brush* to paint his house.

bucket 〔'bʌkɪt 〕 *n.* 水桶 (= *pail*)
Pat carries water with his small *bucket*.

buffet 〔 bʌ'fe 〕 *n.* 自助餐
They had a *buffet* at the wedding.

bug 〔 bʌg 〕 *n.* 小蟲
A ladybug is a beautiful *bug*.

build 〔 bɪld 〕 *v.* 建造
They can *build* a house in one week.

building 〔'bɪldɪŋ 〕 *n.* 建築物
The *building* has 42 floors.

bun 〔 bʌn 〕 *n.* 小圓麵包
I love to eat *buns*.

bundle 〔'bʌndl̩ 〕 *n.* 一大堆
I have a *bundle* of clothes to wash.

burger 〔'bɝgɚ 〕 *n.* 漢堡 (= *hamburger*)
Burgers are my favorite food.

burn 〔 bɝn 〕 *v.* 燃燒
In winter, people *burn* wood to keep warm.

burst〔bɜst〕v. 爆破
My sister's balloon *burst*.

bus〔bʌs〕n. 公車
Joan takes a *bus* to school every day.

business〔'bɪznɪs〕n. 生意
We didn't do much *business* with the firm.

businessman〔'bɪznɪs,mæn〕n. 商人
My father is a *businessman*.

busy〔'bɪzɪ〕adj. 忙碌的
My father is *busy* with his work.

but〔bʌt〕conj. 但是
She would like to go to the party *but* she can't.

butter〔'bʌtɚ〕n. 奶油
Mom put some *butter* in the corn soup.

butterfly〔'bʌtɚ,flaɪ〕n. 蝴蝶
A *butterfly* is an insect with wings full of
bright colors.

button〔'bʌtn̩〕n. 按鈕
I pushed the *button* to turn on the light.

buy〔baɪ〕*v.* 買

Tim went to the supermarket to *buy* food.

by〔baɪ〕*prep.* 搭乘

Mike goes to school *by* bus.

C c

cabbage〔'kæbɪdʒ〕*n.* 包心菜

Joe hates to eat *cabbage*.

cabinet〔'kæbənɪt〕*n.* 櫥櫃

He bought a filing *cabinet* last month.

cable〔'kebḷ〕*n.* 電纜

Cable TV has become more and more popular.

cafeteria〔ˌkæfə'tɪrɪə〕*n.* 自助餐廳

There is a *cafeteria* in our school.

cage〔kedʒ〕*n.* 籠子

There are two lions in the *cage*.

cake〔kek〕*n.* 蛋糕

Chocolate *cake* is my favorite dessert.

calendar (ˈkæləndɚ) *n.* 日曆
Do you have next year's *calendar*?

call (kɔl) *v.* 打電話給～
I will *call* my mother at her office.

calm (kɑm) *adj.* 冷靜的
They were *calm* in the face of the disaster.

camera (ˈkæmərə) *n.* 照相機
Lisa used a *camera* to take pictures of her
friends.

camp (kæmp) *v.* 露營
We will *camp* in the park tonight.

campus (ˈkæmpəs) *n.* 校園
The students are running around the *campus*.

can (kæn) *aux.* 能夠
Wendy *can* type 80 words per minute.

Canada (ˈkænədə) *n.* 加拿大
She comes from *Canada*.

Canadian (kəˈnedɪən) *adj.* 加拿大的
He graduated from a *Canadian* high school.

cancel ('kænsḷ) *v.* 取消

Mr. Jackson *cancelled* his order for the books.

cancer ('kænsɚ) *n.* 癌症

My aunt died of *cancer*.

candle ('kændḷ) *n.* 蠟燭

Michelle has twelve *candles* on her birthday cake.

candy ('kændɪ) *n.* 糖果 (= *sweet*【英式用法】)

You eat too much *candy*.

cap (kæp) *n.* (無邊的) 帽子

Don't forget to wear a *cap* if you go out in the sun.

captain ('kæptɪn) *n.* 隊長;船長

He is the *captain* of our team.

car (kɑr) *n.* 汽車

Tom drives an old *car*.

card (kɑrd) *n.* 卡片

Danny sent a Christmas *card* to me.

care ﹝ kɛr ﹞ v. 在乎
I don't *care* what happens.

career ﹝ kəˈrɪr ﹞ n. 職業
She abandoned her stage *career*.

careful ﹝ ˈkɛrfəl ﹞ adj. 小心的
Be *careful* when you drive the car.

careless ﹝ ˈkɛrlɪs ﹞ adj. 粗心的
It was *careless* of you to lose my keys.

carpet ﹝ ˈkɑrpɪt ﹞ n. 地毯
A cat was sleeping on a *carpet*.

carrot ﹝ ˈkærət ﹞ n. 胡蘿蔔
We grow *carrots* in our garden.

carry ﹝ ˈkærɪ ﹞ v. 攜帶
Linda *carried* a big box.

cartoon ﹝ kɑrˈtun ﹞ n. 卡通
My children enjoy *cartoons*.

case ﹝ kes ﹞ n. 情況
That's a very unusual *case*.

cash ﹝kæʃ﹞ *n.* 現金

Roy pays *cash* for his clothes.

cassette ﹝kæ'sɛt﹞ *n.* 卡式錄音帶

I bought a lot of *cassettes* yesterday.

castle ﹝'kæsḷ﹞ *n.* 城堡

Long ago, kings lived in *castles*.

cat ﹝kæt﹞ *n.* 貓

Many people keep *cats* as pets.

catch ﹝kætʃ﹞ *v.* 捕捉

Jenny keeps a cat to *catch* mice.

cause ﹝kɔz﹞ *n.* 原因

What was the *cause* of the accident?

CD ﹝'si'di﹞ *n.* 唱片 (= *compact disk*)

Mary bought several *CDs* last week.

ceiling ﹝'silɪŋ﹞ *n.* 天花板

A lamp is hanging from the *ceiling*.

celebrate ﹝'sɛlə‚bret﹞ *v.* 慶祝

We *celebrated* Judy's birthday yesterday.

cell ﹝sɛl﹞ *n.* 細胞
All animals are made of *cells*.

cell phone *n.* 手機
We can talk on a *cell phone* at any time.

cent ﹝sɛnt﹞ *n.* 一分錢
There are 100 *cents* to a dollar.

center ﹝'sɛntɚ﹞ *n.* 中心（= *centre*【英式用法】）
New York is a *center* of trade.

centimeter ﹝'sɛntə,mitɚ﹞ *n.* 公分
（= *centimetre*【英式用法】）
Children under 110 *centimeters* need not
pay any fare.

central ﹝'sɛntrəl﹞ *adj.* 中央的
The railroad station is in the *central* part
of the city.

century ﹝'sɛntʃərɪ﹞ *n.* 世紀
We live in the twenty-first *century*.

cereal ﹝'sɪrɪəl﹞ *n.* 穀物食品；早餐食品
I've just bought a box of *cereal*.

certain 〔ˈsɝtn̩ 〕 *adj.* 確定的

I am not *certain* whether he will come today.

certainly 〔ˈsɝtn̩lɪ 〕 *adv.* 必定

She will *certainly* become ill if she goes on working like that.

chair 〔 tʃɛr 〕 *n.* 椅子

I like to sit in a comfortable *chair* while watching TV.

chairman 〔ˈtʃɛrmən 〕 *n.* 主席

He was *chairman* of the meeting.

chalk 〔 tʃɔk 〕 *n.* 粉筆

My teacher is writing with a piece of *chalk*.

chance 〔 tʃæns 〕 *n.* 機會

At the party every child has a *chance* to win a prize.

change 〔 tʃendʒ 〕 *v.* 改變

I will not *change* my mind.

channel 〔ˈtʃænl̩ 〕 *n.* 頻道

What's on *Channel* 55 tonight?

chapter ('tʃæptə) *n.* 章
The book consists of ten *chapters*.

character ('kærɪktə) *n.* 性格
She has a changeable *character*.

charge (tʃɑrdʒ) *v.* 收費
He *charged* me five dollars for a cup of coffee.

chart (tʃɑrt) *n.* 圖表
The result is shown on *chart* 2.

chase (tʃes) *v.* 追
A dog was *chasing* a motorcycle.

cheap (tʃip) *adj.* 便宜的
Everything is *cheap* at that supermarket.

cheat (tʃit) *v.* 欺騙
Kim was *cheated* by the stranger.

check (tʃɛk) *v.* 檢查
Please *check* the door before going to bed.

cheer (tʃɪr) *v.* 使高興
Going to a KTV after the exam will *cheer* me up.

cheese 〔tʃiz〕 *n.* 乳酪；起司

I'm fond of French *cheese*.

chemical 〔'kɛmɪkl̩〕 *adj.* 化學的

Joe decided to be a *chemical* engineer.

chemistry 〔'kɛmɪstrɪ〕 *n.* 化學

I seldom get good grades in *chemistry*.

chess 〔tʃɛs〕 *n.* 西洋棋

My younger brother loves playing *chess*.

chicken 〔'tʃɪkən〕 *n.* 雞肉

I like to eat fried *chicken*.

chief 〔tʃif〕 *adj.* 主要的

What are the *chief* rivers of China?

child 〔tʃaɪld〕 *n.* 小孩（單數）

My aunt has only one *child*.

childhood 〔'tʃaɪld،hʊd〕 *n.* 童年

Her early *childhood* had been very happy.

childish 〔'tʃaɪldɪʃ〕 *adj.* 幼稚的

It's *childish* of you to say that.

childlike ('tʃaɪld,laɪk) *adj.* 天真的
She looked at me with her *childlike* eyes.

chin (tʃɪn) *n.* 下巴
John fell down and broke his *chin*.

China ('tʃaɪnə) *n.* 中國
China is a big country.

Chinese (tʃaɪ'niz) *n.* 中國人
The *Chinese* are a friendly people.

chocolate ('tʃɔkəlɪt) *n.* 巧克力
My sister made a *chocolate* cake yesterday.

choice (tʃɔɪs) *n.* 選擇
Be careful in your *choice* of friends.

choose (tʃuz) *v.* 選擇
Sally has to *choose* the dress she likes best.

chopsticks ('tʃɑp,stɪks) *n.pl.* 筷子
Most Asians eat with *chopsticks*.

Christmas ('krɪsməs) *n.* 聖誕節 (= *Xmas*)
Christmas is on the 25th of December.

chubby (ˈtʃʌbɪ) *adj.* 圓胖的
Daisy has a *chubby* face.

church (tʃɝtʃ) *n.* 教堂
People go to *church* to pray.

circle (ˈsɝkḷ) *n.* 圓圈
Peter drew a *circle* in my book.

citizen (ˈsɪtəzn̩) *n.* 公民
Many Chinese in the United States have
become American *citizens*.

city (ˈsɪtɪ) *n.* 城市
Paris is the capital *city* of France.

claim (klem) *v.* 宣稱
He *claimed* his answer was correct.

clap (klæp) *v.* 拍手
Alice *clapped* when the music ended.

class (klæs) *n.* 班級
There are thirty students in our *class*.

classic (ˈklæsɪk) *adj.* 經典的
Pride and Prejudice is a *classic* work.

classical (ˈklæsɪkḷ) *adj.* 古典的
My mother loves *classical* music.

classmate (ˈklæsˌmet) *n.* 同班同學
Robbie and I have been *classmates* for two years.

classroom (ˈklæsˌrum) *n.* 教室
What are you doing in the *classroom*?

clean (klin) *adj.* 乾淨的
The air is not *clean* in big cities.

clear (klɪr) *adj.* 清楚的
The sea is so *clear* that I can see the fish.

clerk (klɜk) *n.* 店員
My mother works as a *clerk* in the shop.

clever (ˈklɛvɚ) *adj.* 聰明的
He seems to have a lot of *clever* ideas.

climate (ˈklaɪmɪt) *n.* 氣候
She doesn't like to live in a hot *climate*.

climb (klaɪm) *v.* 爬
We will *climb* Mt. Jade this summer.

clock〔klɑk〕*n.* 鐘
I'm going to buy a new *clock* this weekend.

close〔kloz〕*v.* 關上 〔klos〕*adj.* 接近的
Close the door, please.
The population of the city is *close* to a million.

closet〔ˈklɑzɪt〕*n.* 衣櫥
Hang your coat in the *closet*.

clothes〔kloðz〕*n. pl.* 衣服
We need cloth to make *clothes*.

cloud〔klaʊd〕*n.* 雲
The top of Mt. Ali was covered with *clouds*.

cloudy〔ˈklaʊdɪ〕*adj.* 多雲的
Today is a *cloudy* day.

club〔klʌb〕*n.* 俱樂部；社團
Jessica belongs to the drama *club*.

coach〔kotʃ〕*n.* 教練
Ted is my swimming *coach*.

coast〔kost〕*n.* 海岸
They live on the *coast*.

coat〔kot〕*n.* 外套
Everybody likes to wear a *coat* in the winter.

cockroach〔'kɑk,rotʃ〕*n.* 蟑螂（= *roach*）
Lucy is afraid of *cockroaches*.

coffee〔'kɔfɪ〕*n.* 咖啡
I like to drink *coffee* with milk.

coin〔kɔɪn〕*n.* 硬幣
My father's hobby is collecting *coins*.

Coke〔kok〕*n.* 可口可樂（= *Coca-Cola*）
I would like to have a *Coke*.

cold〔kold〕*adj.* 寒冷的
We had a *cold* winter.

collect〔kə'lɛkt〕*v.* 收集
Why do you *collect* dolls?

collection〔kə'lɛkʃən〕*n.* 收集
The *collection* of these stamps took ten years.

college〔'kɑlɪdʒ〕*n.* 大學；學院
What do you plan to do after *college*?

color 〔ˈkʌlə〕 *n.* 顏色 (= *colour*【英式用法】)

My favorite *color* is blue.

colorful 〔ˈkʌləfəl〕 *adj.* 多彩多姿的
(= *colourful*【英式用法】)

In order to live a *colorful* life, you have to
make some changes to your life.

comb 〔kom〕 *n.* 梳子

We use a *comb* to make our hair tidy.

come 〔kʌm〕 *v.* 來

Mr. Brown *comes* to New York every summer.

comfortable 〔ˈkʌmfətəbḷ〕 *adj.* 舒適的

This chair doesn't look *comfortable*.

comic 〔ˈkɑmɪk〕 *adj.* 漫畫的

Ted loves reading *comic* books.

command 〔kəˈmænd〕 *v.* 命令

The captain *commanded* his men to start
at once.

comment 〔ˈkɑmɛnt〕 *n.* 評論

He made no *comment* on the recent topics.

common (ˈkɑmən) *adj.* 常見的
Smith is a very *common* last name in England.

company (ˈkʌmpənɪ) *n.* 公司
Tony worked for this *company* for 18 years.

compare (kəmˈpɛr) *v.* 比較
He *compared* my painting with his.

complain (kəmˈplen) *v.* 抱怨
John is always *complaining*.

complete (kəmˈplit) *adj.* 完成的
His work is *complete*.

computer (kəmˈpjutɚ) *n.* 電腦
Computers are necessary for everyone.

concern (kənˈsɝn) *n.* 關心
He shows no *concern* for his children.

confident (ˈkɑnfədənt) *adj.* 有信心的
He was *confident* that he would win.

confirm (kənˈfɝm) *v.* 證實
This *confirms* my suspicions.

conflict ﹙'kɑnflɪkt﹚ *n.* 衝突
They have a *conflict* in what they believe.

Confucius ﹙kən'fjuʃəs﹚ *n.* 孔子
Confucius is the greatest teacher in Chinese history.

confuse ﹙kən'fjuz﹚ *v.* 使困惑
The new rules *confused* the drivers.

congratulation ﹙kən͵grætʃə'leʃən﹚ *n.* 祝賀
Please accept my *congratulations* on your recovery.

consider ﹙kən'sɪdɚ﹚ *v.* 考慮
Please *consider* my offer.

considerate ﹙kən'sɪdərɪt﹚ *adj.* 體貼的
She is *considerate* to everyone around her.

contact ﹙'kɑntækt﹚ *v.* 聯絡
Contact the police immediately.

contact lens *n.* 隱形眼鏡
Sandy has to wear *contact lenses* when she goes out.

contain ﹝ kən'ten ﹞ v. 包含
Beer *contains* alcohol.

continue ﹝ kən'tɪnju ﹞ v. 繼續
He *continued* to write the novel.

contract ﹝ 'kɑntrækt ﹞ n. 合約
We have a *contract* with that company.

control ﹝ kən'trol ﹞ v. 控制
This plane was *controlled* by the computer
system.

convenience store n. 便利商店
I love to shop in a *convenience store*.

convenient ﹝ kə'vinjənt ﹞ adj. 方便的
Is Friday *convenient* for you?

conversation ﹝ ˌkɑnvə'seʃən ﹞ n. 對話
Mark and Mike are having a *conversation*
over the telephone.

cook ﹝ kʊk ﹞ v. 煮
Jennifer *cooked* noodles for lunch.

cookie ('kʊkɪ) *n.* 餅乾 (= *cooky*)
Sandra is good at making *cookies*.

cool (kul) *adj.* 涼爽的
Please keep the medicine in a *cool* and dry place.

copy ('kɑpɪ) *v.* 影印;抄寫
Copy down the questions in your notebook.

corn (kɔrn) *n.* 玉米
My uncle grows *corn*.

corner ('kɔrnɚ) *n.* 轉角
The post office is right on the *corner*.

correct (kə'rɛkt) *adj.* 正確的
All the answers are *correct*.

cost (kɔst) *v.* 花費
How much will it *cost* to repair this car?

cotton ('kɑtn̩) *n.* 棉
This cloth is made from *cotton*.

couch (kaʊtʃ) *n.* 長沙發
There is a cat on the *couch*.

cough (kɔf) *n.* 咳嗽
The child has a bad *cough*.

could (kʊd) *aux.* can 的過去式
I'm so glad you *could* come.

count (kaʊnt) *v.* 數
My little sister can *count* from 1 to 10.

country ('kʌntrɪ) *n.* 鄉下；國家
I like to live in the *country*.

countryside ('kʌntrɪ,saɪd) *n.* 鄉村地區
The Japanese *countryside* looks its best in
October.

county ('kaʊntɪ) *n.* 縣
Tony wants to move to Taipei *County*.

couple ('kʌpḷ) *n.* 一對
We saw many young *couples* walking in the
park.

courage ('kɜɪdʒ) *n.* 勇氣
He is a man of *courage*.

course ﹝ kors ﹞ *n.* 路線；課程
The airplane changed its *course*.

court ﹝ kort ﹞ *n.* 球場；法庭
Our school has a tennis *court*.

cousin ﹝ˈkʌzn̩﹞ *n.* 堂（表）兄弟姊妹
I have six *cousins* on my mother's side.

cover ﹝ˈkʌvɚ﹞ *v.* 覆蓋
The car is *covered* with snow.

cow ﹝ kaʊ ﹞ *n.* 母牛
You can see *cows* on the farm.

cowboy ﹝ˈkaʊˌbɔɪ﹞ *n.* 牛仔
I'll be a *cowboy* at the party.

crab ﹝ kræb ﹞ *n.* 螃蟹
Crab is my favorite seafood.

crayon ﹝ˈkreən﹞ *n.* 蠟筆
My father sent me a box of *crayons* as my
birthday present.

crazy ﹝ˈkrezɪ﹞ *adj.* 發瘋的；狂熱的
She went *crazy* with fear.

cream ﹝krim﹞ *n.* 奶油；奶精
Do you take *cream* in your coffee?

create ﹝krɪ'et﹞ *v.* 創造
He *created* wonderful characters in his novels.

credit card *n.* 信用卡
My sister has five *credit cards*.

crime ﹝kraɪm﹞ *n.* 罪行
He committed a serious *crime*.

crisis ﹝'kraɪsɪs﹞ *n.* 危機
This country faced a political *crisis*.

cross ﹝krɔs﹞ *v.* 穿越
We *crossed* a lake in a boat.

crowd ﹝kraud﹞ *n.* 群眾
There are *crowds* of people at the market.

crowded ﹝'kraudɪd﹞ *adj.* 擁擠的
The bus was very *crowded*.

cruel ﹝'kruəl﹞ *adj.* 殘忍的
Don't be *cruel* to animals.

cry 〔 kraɪ 〕 *v.* 哭

The little babies always *cry*.

culture 〔 'kʌltʃə 〕 *n.* 文化

Every nation has its own *culture*.

cup 〔 kʌp 〕 *n.* 杯子

I broke my *cup* yesterday.

cure 〔 kjʊr 〕 *v.* 治療

This medicine will *cure* your cold.

curious 〔 'kjʊrɪəs 〕 *adj.* 好奇的

She is too *curious* about other people's business.

current 〔 'kɝənt 〕 *adj.* 現今的；目前的

Our *current* methods of production are too expensive.

curtain 〔 'kɝtn̩ 〕 *n.* 窗簾

We hang *curtains* on our windows.

curve 〔 kɝv 〕 *n.* 曲線

The child drew *curves* on the paper.

custom〔'kʌstəm〕 *n.* 習俗
It's a *custom* for Japanese to bow when they meet their acquaintances.

customer〔'kʌstəmɚ〕 *n.* 顧客
The store has a lot of *customers*.

cut〔kʌt〕 *v.* 切割
She *cut* her finger with a knife.

cute〔kjut〕 *adj.* 可愛的
She is such a *cute* girl.

D d

dad〔dæd〕 *n.* 爸爸
(= *daddy* = *papa* = *pa* = *pop*)
Dad told me a strange story.

daddy〔'dædɪ〕 *n.* 爸爸
Peter is those children's *daddy*.

daily〔'delɪ〕 *adj.* 每天的
I am paid on a *daily* basis.

damage〔'dæmɪdʒ〕 *v.* 損害
The storm *damaged* hundreds of houses.

dance 〔 dæns 〕 v. 跳舞
We can *dance* at the party tomorrow.

danger 〔'dendʒɚ〕 n. 危險
A jungle is full of *danger*.

dangerous 〔'dendʒərəs〕 adj. 危險的
The river is *dangerous* to cross.

dark 〔 dɑrk 〕 adj. 暗的
The house is very *dark* at night.

data 〔'detə〕 n. pl. 資料
（單數為 datum 〔'detəm〕）
Thank you for giving me the *data*.

date 〔 det 〕 n. 日期
What is your *date* of birth?

daughter 〔'dɔtɚ〕 n. 女兒
Lucy is the only *daughter* of the family.

dawn 〔 dɔn 〕 n. 黎明
We set out at *dawn*.

day ﹝ de ﹞ *n.* 天；日子
What *day* is today?

dead ﹝ dɛd ﹞ *adj.* 死的
Susan found a *dead* cat in her house.

deaf ﹝ dɛf ﹞ *adj.* 聾的
He is unable to hear you because he is *deaf*.

deal ﹝ dil ﹞ *v.* 處理
I'm busy, and there are still a lot of things
that I have to *deal* with.

dear ﹝ dɪr ﹞ *adj.* 親愛的
Alice is my *dear* friend.

death ﹝ dɛθ ﹞ *n.* 死亡
Her *death* was a shock to him.

debate ﹝ dɪ'bet ﹞ *v.* 辯論
We are *debating* what to do.

debt ﹝ dɛt ﹞ *n.* 債
If they paid me their *debts*, I should be quite
well off.

December ﹝ dɪ'sɛmbɚ ﹞ *n.* 十二月 ﹙ = *Dec.* ﹚
December is the last month of the year.

decide 〔 dɪˈsaɪd 〕 v. 決定

She has *decided* to marry him.

decision 〔 dɪˈsɪdʒən 〕 n. 決定

I think you've made the wrong *decision*.

decorate 〔ˈdɛkəˌret 〕 v. 裝飾

The hotel room was *decorated* with flowers.

decrease 〔 dɪˈkris 〕 v. 減少

We should *decrease* the amount of our trash.

deep 〔 dip 〕 adj. 深的

The ocean is very *deep*.

deer 〔 dɪr 〕 n. 鹿

A *deer* is an animal with horns.

degree 〔 dɪˈgri 〕 n. 程度

I agree with you to some *degree*.

delay 〔 dɪˈle 〕 v. 使延誤

What *delayed* you so long yesterday?

delicious 〔 dɪˈlɪʃəs 〕 adj. 美味的

What a *delicious* dinner we enjoyed tonight!

deliver ﹝dɪˈlɪvə﹞ v. 遞送
The postman *delivers* letters to our home every day.

democracy ﹝dəˈmɑkrəsɪ﹞ n. 民主政治
You can't have true *democracy* in a one-party state.

democratic ﹝ˌdɛməˈkrætɪk﹞ adj. 民主的
The R.O.C. is a *democratic* country.

dentist ﹝ˈdɛntɪst﹞ n. 牙醫
A *dentist* looks after your teeth.

deny ﹝dɪˈnaɪ﹞ v. 否認
The prisoner *denied* the charges against him.

department ﹝dɪˈpɑrtmənt﹞ n. 部門；科系
Eddie teaches in the literature *department*.

department store n. 百貨公司
I'm on my way to the *department store*.

depend ﹝dɪˈpɛnd﹞ v. 依賴
You cannot *depend* on your parents forever.

describe (dɪ'skraɪb) v. 描述
He was *described* as being very clever.

desert ('dɛzət) n. 沙漠   (dɪ'zɜt) v. 拋棄
There are many camels in the *desert*.
Ray *deserted* his wife and children.

design (dɪ'zaɪn) v. 設計
Adam *designs* clothes for me.

desire (dɪ'zaɪr) v. 想要
What do you *desire* me to do?

desk (dɛsk) n. 書桌
My grandfather made this *desk* for me.

dessert (dɪ'zɜt) n. 餐後甜點
After dinner, we had cake for *dessert*.

detect (dɪ'tɛkt) v. 查出
He soon *detected* the problem.

determine (dɪ'tɜmɪn) v. 決定
He *determined* to return home at once.

develop ﹝dɪ'vɛləp﹞ v. 發展
His business *developed* quickly.

dial ﹝'daɪəl﹞ v. 撥號
I must have *dialed* the wrong number.

diamond ﹝'daɪəmənd﹞ n. 鑽石
Diamonds are a girl's best friend.

diary ﹝'daɪərɪ﹞ n. 日記
I always write in my *diary* at night.

dictionary ﹝'dɪkʃən‚ɛrɪ﹞ n. 字典
Cindy looks up every word in the *dictionary*.

did ﹝dɪd﹞ aux. do 的過去式
Did you go to the party last night?

die ﹝daɪ﹞ v. 死
My grandmother *died* in 1998.

diet ﹝'daɪət﹞ n. 飲食；節食
I'm a little overweight. I need to go on
a *diet*.

difference〔'dɪfərəns〕*n.* 不同

What is the *difference* between a lemon and a lime?

different〔'dɪfərənt〕*adj.* 不同的

A girl is *different* from a boy.

difficult〔'dɪfə‚kʌlt〕*adj.* 困難的

English is not too *difficult* to learn.

difficulty〔'dɪfə‚kʌltɪ〕*n.* 困難

I have *difficulty* remembering names.

dig〔dɪg〕*v.* 挖

The gardener has to *dig* a hole to plant a tree.

diligent〔'dɪlədʒənt〕*adj.* 勤勉的

He is *diligent* in his studies.

dining room *n.* 飯廳

Have we got any coffee in the *dining room*?

dinner〔'dɪnɚ〕*n.* 晚餐

I would like to eat noodles for *dinner*.

dinosaur〔'daɪnə‚sɔr〕*n.* 恐龍

He is interested in *dinosaur*s.

diplomat ('dɪplə,mæt) *n.* 外交官
I want to be a *diplomat* in the future.

direct (də'rɛkt) *v.* 指導；管理
A policeman is *directing* the traffic.

direction (də'rɛkʃən) *n.* 方向
I don't have a sense of *direction*.

director (də'rɛktə) *n.* 導演
Ang Lee is a famous *director*.

dirty ('dɜtɪ) *adj.* 髒的
Allen washed all his *dirty* clothes last night.

disappear (,dɪsə'pɪr) *v.* 消失
The black cat *disappeared* in the dark.

discover (dɪ'skʌvə) *v.* 發現
David *discovered* a stream near the lake.

discuss (dɪ'skʌs) *v.* 討論
Let's sit down to *discuss* this matter, OK?

discussion (dɪ'skʌʃən) *n.* 討論
We had a *discussion* on that issue.

dish 〔 dɪʃ 〕 *n.* 盤子
Used *dishes* are put in the sink.

dishonest 〔 dɪs'ɑnɪst 〕 *adj.* 不誠實的
He is a *dishonest* man.

distance 〔'dɪstəns 〕 *n.* 距離
It is a long *distance* from Taipei to New York.

distant 〔'dɪstənt 〕 *adj.* 遙遠的
The sun is *distant* from the earth.

divide 〔 də'vaɪd 〕 *v.* 劃分
Mom *divided* the pizza into four pieces for us
to share.

division 〔 də'vɪʒən 〕 *n.* 除法
Thirty divided by five is a simple *division*.

dizzy 〔'dɪzɪ 〕 *adj.* 頭暈的
When he got up, he felt *dizzy*.

do 〔 du 〕 *v.* 做   *aux.* (助動詞)
I *do* my homework every day.
Do you love me?

doctor ('dɑktɚ) *n.* 醫生
(= *Dr.* = *doc* = *physician*)
She went to see the *doctor* at two o'clock.

document ('dɑkjəmənt) *n.* 文件
My father is writing out a *document*.

dodge ball *n.* 躲避球
I love to play *dodge ball*.

does (dʌz) *aux.* do 的第三人稱
What *does* he want to drink?

dog (dɔg) *n.* 狗
We keep two *dogs* at home.

doll (dɑl) *n.* 洋娃娃
Most girls like to play with *dolls*.

dollar ('dɑlɚ) *n.* 元 (= *buck*)
One *dollar* is the same as 100 cents.

dolphin ('dɑlfɪn) *n.* 海豚
Most *dolphins* are friendly to people.

done (dʌn) *adj.* 完成的 *aux.* do 的過去分詞
I'll go home when my job is *done*.

donkey ('daŋkɪ) *n.* 驢子
Don't be dumb like a *donkey*.

door (dor) *n.* 門
Please lock the *door* when you come in.

dot (dat) *n.* 點
Her skirt is green with red *dots*.

double ('dʌbl̩) *adj.* 兩倍的
His income is *double* what it was last year.

Double Tenth Day *n.* 雙十節
Jerry was born on *Double Tenth Day*.

doubt (daʊt) *v.* 懷疑
I *doubt* that he will succeed.

doughnut ('do͵nʌt) *n.* 甜甜圈 (= *donut*)
Doughnuts are children's favorite dessert.

down (daʊn) *adv.* 向下地
The children are running up and *down* the stairs.

downstairs ('daʊn'stɛrz) *adv.* 到樓下
He fell *downstairs* and broke his leg.

downtown (ˈdaʊnˈtaʊn) *adv.* 到市中心
We went *downtown* to buy some new clothes.

dozen (ˈdʌzn̩) *n.* 一打
Karen has a *dozen* roses.

Dr. (ˈdɑktɚ) *n.* 博士;醫生 (= *Dr*【英式用法】)
Dr. Lee is a very nice person.

dragon (ˈdrægən) *n.* 龍
In fairy tales, *dragons* are dangerous animals.

Dragon Boat Festival *n.* 端午節
In China, the *Dragon Boat Festival* is a big
day.

drama (ˈdrɑmə) *n.* 戲劇
He wrote many great *dramas*.

draw (drɔ) *v.* 畫
Amy is *drawing* a tree with a pencil.

drawer (drɔr) *n.* 抽屜
I put the book in the left-hand *drawer*.

dream (drim) *n.* 夢
Ben woke up because he had a bad *dream*.

dress 〔 drɛs 〕 *n.* 洋裝
Linda ironed her *dress* before wearing it.

dresser 〔'drɛsɚ〕 *n.* 梳妝台
There are three books on the *dresser*.

drink 〔 drɪŋk 〕 *v.* 喝
I *drink* water when I am thirsty.

drive 〔 draɪv 〕 *v.* 開車
After working, Bob *drove* home.

driver 〔'draɪvɚ〕 *n.* 駕駛人
Sam is a careful *driver*.

drop 〔 drɑp 〕 *v.* 掉落
The book *dropped* from the desk to the floor.

drugstore 〔'drʌg,stor〕 *n.* 藥房
You can buy aspirin at the *drugstore*.

drum 〔 drʌm 〕 *n.* 鼓
Vincent is playing the *drums* in his bedroom.

dry 〔 draɪ 〕 *adj.* 乾的
When Joan arrived, her umbrella was wet
but her clothes were *dry*.

dryer (ˈdraɪɚ) *n.* 烘乾機;吹風機
She bought a new hair *dryer*.

duck (dʌk) *n.* 鴨子
Alice is feeding the *ducks* in the pond.

dumb (dʌm) *adj.* 啞的
He can't answer your question because he is *dumb*.

dumpling (ˈdʌmplɪŋ) *n.* 水餃
We had *dumplings* for dinner last night.

during (ˈdjʊrɪŋ) *prep.* 在…期間
Albert always sleeps *during* class.

duty (ˈdjutɪ) *n.* 責任
The *duty* of a student is to study.

E e

each (itʃ) *adj.* 每一個
Each student in the class got a present.

eagle (ˈigl̩) *n.* 老鷹
Eagles do not breed doves.

ear 〔 ɪr 〕 *n.* 耳朵

We hear with our *ears*.

early 〔'ɝlɪ 〕 *adv.* 早

Most students get up *early* in the morning.

earn 〔 ɝn 〕 *v.* 賺

How much do you *earn* a week?

earrings 〔'ɪr͵rɪŋz 〕 *n. pl.* 耳環

How much do you think he paid for the *earrings*?

earth 〔 ɝθ 〕 *n.* 地球

We live on the *earth*.

ease 〔 iz 〕 *n.* 容易；輕鬆

He solved the math problem with *ease*.

east 〔 ist 〕 *n.* 東方

The sun rises in the *east*.

Easter 〔'istɚ 〕 *n.* 復活節

Easter Day is coming.

eastern 〔'istɚn 〕 *adj.* 東方的

Hualian is on the *eastern* side of Taiwan.

easy (ˈizɪ) *adj.* 容易的
Finishing the work in an hour is not *easy*.

eat (it) *v.* 吃
Do you have something to *eat*?

edge (ɛdʒ) *n.* 邊緣
The *edge* of the plate was broken.

education (ˌɛdʒʊˈkeʃən) *n.* 教育
She received a good *education*.

effect (əˈfɛkt, ɪˈfɛkt) *n.* 影響;效果
The accident had a direct *effect* on us.
This medicine had a miraculous *effect*.

effective (əˈfɛktɪv) *adj.* 有效的
The pills were *effective* in stopping my cough.

effort (ˈɛfət) *n.* 努力
We can do nothing without *effort*.

egg (ɛg) *n.* 蛋
I had fried rice and *eggs* for breakfast.

eight 〔 et 〕 *n.* 八

Four plus four is *eight*.

eighteen 〔 e'tin 〕 *n.* 十八

Mark has worked in a bank since he was *eighteen*.

eighteenth 〔'e'tinθ 〕 *adj.* 第十八個

He is the *eighteenth* guest.

eighth 〔 etθ 〕 *adj.* 第八的

Today is the *eighth* of August.

eighty 〔'etɪ 〕 *adj.* 八十個

There are *eighty* people in the room.

either 〔'iðə 〕 *adj.* 兩者之一的

I don't have *either* a cat or a dog.

elder 〔'ɛldə 〕 *adj.* 年長的

She is my *elder* sister.

elect 〔 ɪ'lɛkt 〕 *v.* (以投票) 選出

We *elected* him as our mayor.

election (ɪˈlɛkʃən) *n.* 選舉
He was elected to the Senate in the last *election*.

electric (ɪˈlɛktrɪk) *adj.* 電的
The *electric* light went out.

element (ˈɛləmənt) *n.* 要素
Love is an *element* of kindness.

elementary school *n.* 小學
(= *primary school*)
He didn't finish *elementary school*.

elephant (ˈɛləfənt) *n.* 大象
Elephants are found in Asia and Africa.

eleven (ɪˈlɛvən) *n.* 十一
Eleven comes after the number ten.

eleventh (ɪˈlɛvənθ) *adj.* 第十一的
Yesterday was the *eleventh* of May.

else (ɛls) *adj.* 別的；其他的
What *else* can I do?

e-mail 〔'i,mel 〕 *n.* 電子郵件
You can contact me by *e-mail*.

embarrass 〔 ɪm'bærəs 〕 *v.* 使尷尬
Your question did *embarrass* me. I don't
want to answer it.

emotion 〔 ɪ'moʃən 〕 *n.* 情緒
Love, joy and hate are all *emotions*.

emphasize 〔'ɛmfə,saɪz 〕 *v.* 強調
(= *emphasise* 【英式用法】)
Which word should I *emphasize*?

employ 〔 ɪm'plɔɪ 〕 *v.* 雇用
The company *employs* 500 workers.

empty 〔'ɛmptɪ 〕 *adj.* 空的
The box was *empty*.

encourage 〔 ɪn'kɝɪdʒ 〕 *v.* 鼓勵
Your letter *encouraged* me greatly.

end 〔 ɛnd 〕 *n.* 末尾；結束
Sara arrived home at the *end* of last week.

enemy (ˈɛnəmɪ) *n.* 敵人
He has many *enemies* in the political world.

energetic (ˌɛnəˈdʒɛtɪk) *adj.* 充滿活力的
He is young and *energetic*.

energy (ˈɛnədʒɪ) *n.* 活力
He has amazing *energy*.

engine (ˈɛndʒən) *n.* 引擎
This car has a new *engine*.

engineer (ˌɛndʒəˈnɪr) *n.* 工程師
The car was designed by *engineers*.

England (ˈɪŋglənd) *n.* 英國
I've never been to *England*.

English (ˈɪŋglɪʃ) *n.* 英語
Ellen studies *English* every Sunday.

Englishman (ˈɪŋglɪʃmən) *n.* 英國人
James is an *Englishman*.

enjoy (ɪnˈdʒɔɪ) *v.* 享受；喜歡
How did you *enjoy* your trip?

enough 〔 ə'nʌf 〕 *adj.* 足夠的
Have you got *enough* money to pay for this
meal?

enter 〔'ɛntɚ 〕 *v.* 進入
Don't *enter* the room!

entire 〔 ɪn'taɪr 〕 *adj.* 全部的
I was in *entire* ignorance of what had happened.

entrance 〔'ɛntrəns 〕 *n.* 入口
We used the back *entrance* to the building.

envelope 〔'ɛnvə,lop 〕 *n.* 信封
Nancy forgot to write the address on the
envelope.

environment 〔 ɪn'vaɪrənmənt 〕 *n.* 環境
The *environment* here is good.

envy 〔'ɛnvɪ 〕 *n.* 羨慕
She looked at Mary's diamond ring with *envy*.

equal 〔'ikwəl 〕 *adj.* 相等的
Men and women have *equal* rights.

eraser (ɪ'resɚ) *n.* 橡皮擦
My mother bought me a new *eraser*.

error ('ɛrɚ) *n.* 錯誤
There are too many *errors* in his report.

especially (ə'spɛʃəlɪ) *adv.* 特別地
It's *especially* cold today.

Europe ('jʊrəp) *n.* 歐洲
Jennifer plans to travel to *Europe* during
summer vacation.

European (͵jʊrə'piən) *adj.* 歐洲的
France is a *European* country.

eve (iv) *n.* 前夕
Christmas *Eve* is a happy time for children.

even ('ivən) *adv.* 甚至
I have no money. I can't *even* ride the bus.

evening ('ivnɪŋ) *n.* 傍晚
The sun sets in the *evening*.

event (ɪ'vɛnt) *n.* 事件；大事
His visit was quite an *event*.

ever (ˈɛvɚ) *adv.* 曾經
Have you *ever* seen a lion?

every (ˈɛvrɪ) *adj.* 每一
I get up at six *every* morning.

everybody (ˈɛvrɪˌbɑdɪ) *pron.* 每個人
Everybody knows him as a singer.

everyone (ˈɛvrɪˌwʌn) *pron.* 每個人
(= *everybody*)
Everyone wants to attend the concert.

everything (ˈɛvrɪˌθɪŋ) *pron.* 一切事物
How is *everything*?

everywhere (ˈɛvrɪˌhwɛr) *adv.* 到處
I can go *everywhere* with my car.

evil (ˈivl̩) *adj.* 邪惡的
The old witch was *evil*.

exact (ɪgˈzækt) *adj.* 準確的
Your description is not very *exact*.

exam (ɪgˈzæm) *n.* 考試
Students have to take a lot of *exams*.

examine 〔 ɪgˈzæmɪn 〕 *v.* 檢查
He *examined* the room.

example 〔 ɪgˈzæmpḷ 〕 *n.* 例子
Here is another *example*.

excellent 〔ˈɛksḷənt 〕 *adj.* 優秀的
He has an *excellent* memory.

except 〔 ɪkˈsɛpt 〕 *prep.* 除了…之外
I like all animals *except* snakes.

excite 〔 ɪkˈsaɪt 〕 *v.* 使興奮
The movie *excited* us.

excited 〔 ɪkˈsaɪtɪd 〕 *adj.* 興奮的
Why are you so *excited* today?

exciting 〔 ɪkˈsaɪtɪŋ 〕 *adj.* 令人興奮的
What an *exciting* race it was!

excuse 〔 ɪkˈskjuz 〕 *v.* 原諒
Excuse me for what I said to you yesterday.

exercise 〔ˈɛksɚˌsaɪz 〕 *n.* 運動
My father gets a lot of *exercise* every evening.

exist〔 ɪgˈzɪst 〕 v. 存在

Plants cannot *exist* without water.

exit 〔ˈɛgzɪt 〕 n. 出口

When there is a fire, you can run out through the emergency *exit*.

expect 〔 ɪkˈspɛkt 〕 v. 期待

I *expect* to see you tomorrow.

expensive 〔 ɪkˈspɛnsɪv 〕 adj. 昂貴的

A new car is very *expensive*.

experience 〔 ɪkˈspɪrɪəns 〕 n. 經驗

He has no *experience* in teaching English.

expert 〔ˈɛkspɝt 〕 n. 專家

Kelly is an *expert* in economics.

explain 〔 ɪkˈsplen 〕 v. 解釋

Please *explain* this rule to me.

export 〔 ɪksˈport 〕 v. 出口

We now *export* all kinds of industrial products.

express 〔 ɪkˈsprɛs 〕 v. 表達

I don't know how to *express* my thankfulness.

extra ('εkstrə) *adj.* 額外的

I don't need any *extra* help.

eye (aɪ) *n.* 眼睛

I can't take my *eyes* off the game.

eyebrow ('aɪ,braʊ) *n.* 眉毛

He raised an *eyebrow* at the news.

F f

face (fes) *n.* 臉

Look into the mirror and you can see your own *face*.

fact (fækt) *n.* 事實

A *fact* is something that is true.

factory ('fæktrɪ) *n.* 工廠

The children are going to visit a car *factory*.

fail (fel) *v.* 失敗

Our plan has *failed*.

failure ('feljɚ) *n.* 失敗

His *failure* in business was due to his laziness.

fair 〔 fɛr 〕 *adj.* 公平的   *n.* 展覽會

The judge made a *fair* decision.

There will be a book *fair* in January.

fall 〔 fɔl 〕 *v.* 落下   *n.* 秋天 (= *autumn*)

The rain is *falling* down from the sky.

false 〔 fɔls 〕 *adj.* 錯誤的

It was *false* news. Don't believe it.

family 〔'fæməlɪ 〕 *n.* 家庭；家人

How is your *family*?

famous 〔'feməs 〕 *adj.* 有名的

Many people visit the *famous* mountain.

fan 〔 fæn 〕 *n.* 風扇；迷

Nancy needs a new *fan* for this summer.

fancy 〔'fænsɪ 〕 *adj.* 精緻的

My boyfriend invited me to a *fancy* restaurant on Valentine's Day.

fantastic 〔 fæn'tæstɪk 〕 *adj.* 很棒的

She's really a *fantastic* girl.

far (far) *adj.* 遠的
The shop is not *far* from here.

farm (farm) *n.* 農場
People keep animals on a *farm*.

farmer ('farmɚ) *n.* 農夫
Mr. Smith is a *farmer*.

fashionable ('fæʃənəbl̩) *adj.* 時髦的
The hat is so *fashionable* that I can't wait to
try it on.

fast (fæst) *adv.* 快地
Don't drive too *fast*.

fat (fæt) *adj.* 胖的
Her cat is very *fat* because it eats too much.

father ('faðɚ) *n.* 父親 (= *dad*)
Jonathan is a good *father*.

faucet ('fɔsɪt) *n.* 水龍頭
Remember to turn off the *faucet*.

fault (fɔlt) *n.* 過錯
It was his *fault* that the window broke.

favor (ˈfevɚ) *n.* 恩惠；幫助 *v.* 偏愛
(= *favour* 【英式用法】)

May I ask you a *favor*?

She *favored* her youngest son.

favorite (ˈfevərɪt) *adj.* 最喜愛的
(= *favourite* 【英式用法】)

White chocolate is my *favorite* snack.

fear (fɪr) *v.* 害怕

She has always *feared* cats.

February (ˈfɛbruˌɛrɪ) *n.* 二月 (= *Feb.*)

February is the second month of the year.

fee (fi) *n.* 費用

The *fee* to the exhibition is 20 dollars.

feed (fid) *v.* 餵食

We *feed* the birds every day.

feel (fil) *v.* 覺得

I *feel* happy because I am playing with friends.

feeling (ˈfilɪŋ) *n.* 感覺

He lost all *feeling* in his right leg.

fellow ('fεlo) *n.* 同伴
We were *fellows* at school.

female ('fimel) *n.* 女性
There are few *females* working as pilots.

fence (fεns) *n.* 籬笆
That small house doesn't have a *fence*.

festival ('fεstəvḷ) *n.* 節日
Christmas is an important church *festival*.

fever ('fivə) *n.* 發燒
He has a little *fever*.

few (fju) *adj.* 少的
There were *few* people in the streets.

field (fild) *n.* 領域
Many scientists are working in this *field*.

fifteen (fɪf'tin) *n.* 十五
They get their I.D. cards at the age of *fifteen*.

fifteenth (fɪf'tinθ) *adj.* 第十五的
On the *fifteenth* day of a lunar month, many
people come to the temple.

fifth 〔 fɪfθ 〕 *adj.* 第五的

He is the *fifth* person to ask me the question.

fifty 〔'fɪftɪ 〕 *adj.* 五十個

There are *fifty* students in our class.

fight 〔 faɪt 〕 *v.* 打架

Dogs always *fight* with cats.

figure 〔'fɪgjɚ 〕 *n.* 數字

He wrote the date in *figures*.

fill 〔 fɪl 〕 *v.* 裝滿

He *filled* my glass with water.

film 〔 fɪlm 〕 *n.* 電影

Who stars in this *film*?

final 〔'faɪn̩ 〕 *adj.* 最後的

This is your *final* chance.

finally 〔'faɪn̩ɪ 〕 *adv.* 最後

It was difficult, but I *finally* finished the work.

find 〔 faɪnd 〕 *v.* 發現

The doctor can't *find* the cause of his illness.

fine ﹝ faɪn ﹞ *adj.* 美好的   *v.* (對某人) 處以罰金
The weather is *fine*, isn't it?
Will the judge *fine* him heavily?

finger ﹝ 'fɪŋɚ ﹞ *n.* 手指
We have five *fingers* on each hand.

finish ﹝ 'fɪnɪʃ ﹞ *v.* 完成
I'll *finish* this work by nine o'clock.

fire ﹝ faɪr ﹞ *n.* 火
Are you afraid of *fire*?

firm ﹝ fɜm ﹞ *n.* 公司   *adj.* 堅硬的
The *firm* has not been doing well recently.
Exercise made my muscles very *firm*.

first ﹝ fɜst ﹞ *adj.* 第一的
The *first* person to arrive is John.

fish ﹝ fɪʃ ﹞ *n.* 魚
They caught several *fish*.

fisherman ﹝ 'fɪʃəmən ﹞ *n.* 漁夫
A *fisherman* catches fish every day.

fit〔 fɪt 〕*v.* 適合

This skirt does not *fit* me.

five〔 faɪv 〕*adj.* 五個

Children go to school *five* days a week.

fix〔 fɪks 〕*v.* 修理

The machine needs to be *fixed*.

flag〔 flæg 〕*n.* 旗子

There are three colors on our national *flag*.

flashlight〔'flæʃ͵laɪt 〕*n.* 手電筒 (= *flash*)

I need a *flashlight* to help me find my way out.

flat〔 flæt 〕*adj.* 平坦的 *n.* 公寓 (= *apartment*)

The farmland is quite *flat*.

My boss has several blocks of *flats*.

flat tire   *n.* 洩了氣的輪胎

There are two *flat tires* on this car.

flight〔 flaɪt 〕*n.* 飛行；班機

He took the five o'clock *flight* to Tokyo.

floor〔 flor 〕*n.* 地板；樓層

This elevator stops at every *floor*.

flour ﹝ flaʊr ﹞ *n.* 麵粉
Flour is used for making bread.

flow ﹝ flo ﹞ *v.* 流
The water was *flowing* out.

flower ﹝ 'flaʊɚ ﹞ *n.* 花
People give *flowers* on Valentine's Day.

flu ﹝ flu ﹞ *n.* 流行性感冒
He is in bed with the *flu*.

flute ﹝ flut ﹞ *n.* 笛子
Jason asked his mother to buy a *flute* for him.

fly ﹝ flaɪ ﹞ *v.* 飛　*n.* 蒼蠅
A bird *flies* in the sky.
Everybody hates *flies*.

focus ﹝ 'fokəs ﹞ *n.* 焦點
She always wants to be the *focus* of attention.

fog ﹝ fɔg, fɑg ﹞ *n.* 霧
Fog is a cloud near the ground.

foggy ﹝ 'fɑgɪ ﹞ *adj.* 多霧的
Tonight is a *foggy* night.

follow (ˈfɑlo) *v.* 遵守

Students must *follow* rules.

following (ˈfɑləwɪŋ) *adj.* 下列的

Answer the *following* questions.

food (fud) *n.* 食物

Without *food*, people cannot live.

fool (ful) *n.* 傻瓜

He is such a *fool* that he doesn't know what to do.

foolish (ˈfulɪʃ) *adj.* 愚蠢的

It's *foolish* of you to do a thing like that.

foot (fut) *n.* 腳;英呎

Wendy hurt her left *foot*.

football (ˈfut͵bɔl) *n.* 橄欖球

Football is an exciting game.

for (fɔr) *prep.* 給…

This apple is *for* Anne.

force (fɔrs) *v.* 強迫 *n.* 力量

They *forced* him to sign the document.

foreign ('fɔrɪn) *adj.* 外國的
Our new classmate has a *foreign* accent.

foreigner ('fɔrɪnə) *n.* 外國人
For a *foreigner*, your Chinese is pretty good.

forest ('fɔrɪst) *n.* 森林
The monkeys live in a *forest*.

forget (fə'gɛt) *v.* 忘記
Robert *forgot* to bring his book to school.

forgive (fə'gɪv) *v.* 原諒
Mom *forgave* me for stealing her money.

fork (fɔrk) *n.* 叉子
When we eat, we use *forks* and knives.

form (fɔrm) *n.* 表格；形式
Joy forgot to bring an application *form*.

formal ('fɔrml̩) *adj.* 正式的
I wore *formal* clothes to the party.

former ('fɔrmə) *adj.* 從前的 *n.* 前者
They are my *former* students.
The *former* is better than the latter.

forty ('fɔrtɪ) *n.* 四十
Forty comes after the number thirty-nine.

forward ('fɔrwəd) *adv.* 向前
(= *forwards* 【英式用法】)
Go *forward* and you can see the bookstore
on the corner.

four (for) *adj.* 四個
There are *four* people in my family.

fourteen ('for'tin) *adj.* 十四的
Jessie is *fourteen* this year.

fourteenth ('for'tinθ) *adj.* 第十四的
Tomorrow will be the *fourteenth* of June.

fourth (forθ) *adj.* 第四個
You are the *fourth* person to arrive.

fox (faks) *n.* 狐狸
A *fox* is a wild animal.

France (fræns) *n.* 法國
France is next to Germany.

frank (fræŋk) *adj.* 坦白的
He is *frank* with me about everything.

free (fri) *adj.* 免費的；自由的
There is no *free* lunch in this world.

freedom ('fridəm) *n.* 自由
He has *freedom* to do what he likes.

freezer ('frizɚ) *n.* 冰箱
There is a lot of food in our *freezer*.

freezing ('frizɪŋ) *adj.* 極冷的
It's *freezing* cold on high mountaintops.

French (frɛntʃ) *n.* 法語
I can't speak *French*.

French fries *n. pl.* 薯條
I ate three bags of *French fries* today.

fresh (frɛʃ) *adj.* 新鮮的
The cake is very *fresh*.

Friday ('fraɪdɪ) *n.* 星期五 (= *Fri.*)
Friday night is the best time to go out.

fried (fraɪd) *adj.* 油炸的
My mother dislikes eating *fried* chicken.

friend (frɛnd) *n.* 朋友
Everyone needs a *friend* to share his feelings
with.

friendly ('frɛndlɪ) *adj.* 友善的
My teacher is very *friendly* to us.

friendship ('frɛndʃɪp) *n.* 友誼
Our *friendship* will last forever.

frighten ('fraɪtn̩) *v.* 驚嚇
I'm sorry I *frightened* you.

Frisbee ('frɪzbi) *n.* 飛盤
Helen and Nick are playing *Frisbee* in the park.

frog (frɑg) *n.* 青蛙
Frogs are jumping in the rain.

from (frɑm) *prep.* 從…
Andy came *from* Japan.

front (frʌnt) *n.* 前面
Don't park your car in *front* of the building.

fruit ﹝ frut ﹞ *n.* 水果
Strawberries are my favorite *fruit*.

fry ﹝ fraɪ ﹞ *v.* 油炸
She *fried* a fish.

full ﹝ fʊl ﹞ *adj.* 充滿的
This river is *full* of fish.

fun ﹝ fʌn ﹞ *n.* 樂趣
I had so much *fun* at the party last night.

function ﹝ ˋfʌŋkʃən ﹞ *n.* 功能
What is the *function* of the heart?

funny ﹝ ˋfʌnɪ ﹞ *adj.* 好玩的
There's something *funny* about it.

furniture ﹝ ˋfɝnɪtʃɚ ﹞ *n.* 家具
We need some *furniture* for our new house.

further ﹝ ˋfɝðɚ ﹞ *adj.* 更進一步的　*adv.* 更遠
He will need *further* help.
Edward tries to go *further* away.

future ﹝ ˋfjutʃɚ ﹞ *n.* 未來
Ronald will become a doctor in the *future*.

G g

gain 〔 gen 〕 *v.* 獲得；增加
She is *gaining* weight.

game 〔 gem 〕 *n.* 遊戲
Children like to play *games*.

garage 〔 gə'rɑʒ 〕 *n.* 車庫
Tom's parents park their car in the *garage*.

garbage 〔'gɑrbɪdʒ 〕 *n.* 垃圾
We must take out the *garbage* at 9:00.

garden 〔'gɑrdṇ 〕 *n.* 花園
Grandpa usually spends his free time in
the *garden*.

gas 〔 gæs 〕 *n.* 瓦斯
Mother cooks with *gas*.

gasoline 〔'gæslˏin 〕 *n.* 汽油（ = *gas* = *petrol* ）
Gasoline is necessary in our daily life.

gate 〔 get 〕 *n.* 大門
The castle's *gate* is very high.

gather 〔'gæðə〕 v. 聚集
A lot of people *gathered* to see the parade.

general 〔'dʒɛnərəl〕 *adj.* 一般的　*n.* 將軍
Clark gave me a *general* idea of what happened.
Here is the report, *General*.

generation 〔ˌdʒɛnə'reʃən〕 *n.* 世代
Father, son and grandson are three *generations*.

generous 〔'dʒɛnərəs〕 *adj.* 慷慨的
My mother is a *generous* person.

genius 〔'dʒinjəs〕 *n.* 天才
Mark is so smart that he is thought of as a
genius.

gentle 〔'dʒɛntl̩〕 *adj.* 溫和的
Ricky is very *gentle*.

gentleman 〔'dʒɛntl̩mən〕 *n.* 紳士
This *gentleman* wishes to see the manager.

geography 〔dʒi'ɑgrəfɪ〕 *n.* 地理
I am going to have an exam in *geography*
tomorrow.

German (ˈdʒɝmən) *adj.* 德國的
German sausage is very delicious.

Germany (ˈdʒɝmənɪ) *n.* 德國
Germany is Joyce's favorite country.

gesture (ˈdʒɛstʃɚ) *n.* 姿勢
Japanese don't use as many *gestures* as
Americans.

get (gɛt) *v.* 獲得
I hope to *get* some letters from him.

ghost (gost) *n.* 鬼
Do you believe in *ghosts*?

giant (ˈdʒaɪənt) *n.* 巨人；大漢
Jack saw the *giant* climbing down the
beanstalk.

gift (gɪft) *n.* 禮物
I got a *gift* from my teacher.

girl (gɝl) *n.* 女孩
Tina is a very clever *girl*.

give 〔 gɪv 〕 v. 給

Maria *gives* me a present every Christmas.

glad 〔 glæd 〕 *adj.* 高興的

I'm *glad* to see you again.

glass 〔 glæs 〕 *n.* 玻璃杯

Can you give me a *glass* of water, please?

glasses 〔'glæsɪz〕 *n. pl.* 眼鏡

I need *glasses* when I read.

glove 〔 glʌv 〕 *n.* 手套

Baseball players need to wear *gloves*.

glue 〔 glu 〕 *v.* 塗膠水黏貼　*n.* 膠水

She *glued* her pictures on the wall.

go 〔 go 〕 *v.* 去

Justin *goes* to school every day.

goal 〔 gol 〕 *n.* 目標

Getting into university is my *goal*.

goat 〔 got 〕 *n.* 山羊

Goats make funny sounds.

God 〔 gɑd 〕 *n.* 上帝
My *God*! I forgot to lock the door.

gold 〔 gold 〕 *n.* 黃金
Gold is a shiny, yellow metal.

golden 〔'goldn̩ 〕 *adj.* 金色的
Her *golden* ring is beautiful.

golf 〔 gɔlf, gɑlf 〕 *n.* 高爾夫球
Everyone in my family plays *golf*.

good 〔 gʊd 〕 *adj.* 好的
Uncle Andrew is a *good* man.

good-bye 〔 gʊd'baɪ 〕 *interj.* 再見
(= *goodbye* = *bye*)
Good-bye. See you tomorrow.

goodness 〔'gʊdnɪs 〕 *interj.* 天啊
My *goodness*! You are late again!

goose 〔 gus 〕 *n.* 鵝
The farmer is running after the *goose*.

government 〔'gʌvɚnmənt 〕 *n.* 政府
The *government* is responsible to the people.

grade ﹝ gred ﹞ *n.* 成績
Mary always got high *grades* in school.

gram ﹝ græm ﹞ *n.* 公克 (= *g* = *gm* = *gramme*)
Mom asked me to buy 200 *grams* of sugar.

grand ﹝ grænd ﹞ *adj.* 雄偉的
I was deeply struck with the *grand* building.

granddaughter ﹝'grænd͵dɔtɚ﹞ *n.* 孫女
My father has five *granddaughters*.

grandfather ﹝'grænd͵fɑðɚ﹞ *n.* 祖父
(= *grandpa*)
My *grandfather* died when I was young.

grandmother ﹝'grænd͵mʌðɚ﹞ *n.* 祖母
(= *grandma*)
My *grandmother* is still alive.

grandson ﹝'grænd͵sʌn﹞ *n.* 孫子
My mother wants to have a *grandson*.

grape ﹝ grep ﹞ *n.* 葡萄
Wine is made from *grapes*.

grass〔græs〕*n.* 草

It's good to cut the *grass* once a week.

gray〔gre〕*n.* 灰色 (= *grey*)

Gray is the color of an elephant.

great〔gret〕*adj.* 大的

New York is a *great* city.

greedy〔'gridɪ〕*adj.* 貪心的

He is *greedy* to gain power.

green〔grin〕*n.* 綠色

Green is the color of grass.

greet〔grit〕*v.* 和…打招呼

Juniors should *greet* seniors.

ground〔graʊnd〕*n.* 地面

She lay on the *ground*.

group〔grup〕*n.* 團體

In class, we form *groups* to do different things.

grow〔gro〕*v.* 種植

The farmer *grows* vegetables on his farm.

growth 〔 groθ 〕 *n.* 生長
Growth is rapid in infancy.

guard 〔 gɑrd 〕 *n.* 警衛
There are *guards* to look after the building.

guava 〔 'gwɑvə 〕 *n.* 芭樂
Guavas are my favorite fruit.

guess 〔 gɛs 〕 *v.* 猜測
Can you *guess* my age?

guest 〔 gɛst 〕 *n.* 客人
We're expecting *guests* for dinner.

guide 〔 gaɪd 〕 *v.* 指導
Children need to be *guided* in good ways.

guitar 〔 gɪ'tɑr 〕 *n.* 吉他
John plays *guitar* very well.

gun 〔 gʌn 〕 *n.* 槍
He taught Helen how to shoot a *gun*.

guy 〔 gaɪ 〕 *n.* 傢伙；人
Mr. Johnson is a nice *guy*.

gym ﹝ dʒɪm ﹞ *n.* 體育館

We play basketball in a *gym*.

H h

habit ﹝'hæbɪt ﹞ *n.* 習慣

The boy has very good *habits*.

had ﹝ hæd ﹞ *v.* have 的過去式

If I *had* money, I would lend you some.

hair ﹝ hɛr ﹞ *n.* 頭髮

Rose has long black *hair*.

haircut ﹝'hɛr͵kʌt ﹞ *n.* 理髮

I had a *haircut* yesterday.

hairdresser ﹝'hɛr͵drɛsə ﹞ *n.* 美髮師

I went to another *hairdresser*.

half ﹝ hæf ﹞ *n.* 一半

Half of the boys in this room are my friends.

hall ﹝ hɔl ﹞ *n.* 大廳

Your father is waiting for you across
the *hall*.

Halloween (ˌhæloˈin) *n.* 萬聖節前夕
Children are looking forward to the coming of *Halloween*.

ham (hæm) *n.* 火腿
I had *ham* and eggs for my breakfast.

hamburger (ˈhæmbɝgɚ) *n.* 漢堡 (= *burger*)
I think I'll have a *hamburger*.

hammer (ˈhæmɚ) *n.* 鐵鎚
George hit the nail with a *hammer*.

hand (hænd) *n.* 手 *v.* 交給
We use our *hands* to do a lot of things.
He *handed* me a ticket at the entrance.

handkerchief (ˈhæŋkɚtʃɪf) *n.* 手帕
She dropped her *handkerchief*.

handle (ˈhændḷ) *v.* 處理 *n.* 手把
The court has many cases to *handle*.
The *handle* of the suitcase is broken.

handsome (ˈhænsəm) *adj.* 英俊的
Todd is a *handsome* man.

hang 〔 hæŋ 〕 *v.* 懸掛

She *hung* the picture on the wall.

hanger 〔'hæŋɚ〕 *n.* 衣架

How about that coat on the *hanger*?

happen 〔'hæpən〕 *v.* 發生

What will *happen* next?

happy 〔'hæpɪ〕 *adj.* 高興的

Charlie is *happy* to see his mother again.

hard 〔 hɑrd 〕 *adj.* 困難的

It is a *hard* question to answer.

hardly 〔'hɑrdlɪ〕 *adv.* 幾乎不

I can *hardly* believe it.

hard-working 〔'hɑrd'wɝkɪŋ 〕 *adj.* 辛勤的；
用功的

Bob is a *hard-working* person.

has 〔 hæz 〕 *v.* have 的第三人稱單數

Joe *has* his own house near the river.

hat 〔 hæt 〕 *n.* 帽子

My mother bought me a red *hat*.

hate ﹝ het ﹞ *v.* 討厭
My brother *hates* snakes.

have ﹝ hæv ﹞ *v.* 有 *aux.* ﹝助動詞﹞
I *have* two pens and three pencils.
Have you ever eaten this kind of fruit?

he ﹝ hi ﹞ *pron.* 他
He is a teacher in a senior high school.

head ﹝ hɛd ﹞ *n.* 頭
Lucy wears a hat on her *head*.

headache ﹝ˈhɛdˌek﹞ *n.* 頭痛
Sandy has a bad *headache*.

health ﹝ hɛlθ ﹞ *n.* 健康
Nothing is better than having good *health*.

healthy ﹝ˈhɛlθɪ﹞ *adj.* 健康的
Kate's baby is very *healthy*.

hear ﹝ hɪr ﹞ *v.* 聽見
I *heard* the birds singing.

heart ﹝ hɑrt ﹞ *n.* 心
My *heart* always beats very fast after running.

heat 〔 hit 〕 *n.* 熱
The sun gives us *heat* and light.

heater 〔'hitɚ 〕 *n.* 暖氣機
Please turn on the *heater*.

heavy 〔'hɛvɪ 〕 *adj.* 重的
This box is very *heavy*.

height 〔 haɪt 〕 *n.* 高度
The tree grows to a *height* of 20 feet.

helicopter 〔'hɛlɪˌkɑptɚ 〕 *n.* 直昇機
I saw a *helicopter* in the sky.

hello 〔 hə'lo 〕 *interj.* 哈囉
"*Hello*" is a word of greeting.

help 〔 hɛlp 〕 *v.* 幫忙
I love to *help* my mother cook.

helpful 〔'hɛlpfəl 〕 *adj.* 有幫助的
You're very *helpful*.

hen 〔 hɛn 〕 *n.* 母雞
My grandfather raises *hens* in the country.

her 〔 hɝ 〕*adj.* 她的
Her seat is over there.

here 〔 hɪr 〕*adv.* 這裡
There is no one *here* today.

hero 〔'hɪro 〕*n.* 英雄
My father is my *hero*.

hers 〔 hɝz 〕*pron.* she 的所有代名詞
This is not Jane's pen; *hers* is over there.

herself 〔 hɚ'sɛlf 〕*pron.* she 的反身代名詞
She saw *herself* in the mirror.

hey 〔 he 〕*interj.* 嘿
Hey, come and look at this!

hi 〔 haɪ 〕*interj.* 嗨
Hi there.

hide 〔 haɪd 〕*v.* 隱藏
The girl *hides* herself from her mother.

high 〔 haɪ 〕*adj.* 高的
He lives on a *high* floor in that building.

highway 〔'haɪ,we 〕 *n.* 公路
We're driving on the *highway*.

hike 〔 haɪk 〕 *v.* 健行
I go *hiking* every Sunday morning.

hill 〔 hɪl 〕 *n.* 山丘
We climbed a *hill* last Sunday.

him 〔 hɪm 〕 *pron.* he 的受格
Henry told me to wait for *him*.

himself 〔 hɪm'sɛlf 〕 *pron.* he 的反身代名詞
David fell and hurt *himself*.

hip 〔 hɪp 〕 *n.* 臀部
The boy hurt his *hip*.

hippopotamus 〔,hɪpə'patəməs 〕 *n.* 河馬
(= *hippo*)
We can see a lot of *hippopotamuses* in the zoo.

hire 〔 haɪr 〕 *v.* 雇用
He *hired* a workman to paint the wall.

his (hɪz) *adj.* 他的
Can I borrow *his* car?

history ('hɪstrɪ) *n.* 歷史
History is my favorite subject.

hit (hɪt) *v.* 打
He was *hit* by the teacher because he didn't
do his homework.

hobby ('hɑbɪ) *n.* 嗜好
My favorite *hobby* is collecting stamps.

hold (hold) *v.* 拿著
He *holds* the bag with both hands.

hole (hol) *n.* 洞
There is a *hole* in this bowl.

holiday ('hɑlə‚de) *n.* 假日
People don't work or go to school on a
holiday.

home (hom) *adv.* 回家　*n.* 家
My mother usually gets *home* at 10:00.

homesick ('hom,sɪk) *adj.* 想家的

I became *homesick* after a week's stay at my aunt's.

homework ('hom,wɜk) *n.* 作業

Sally cannot go out because she has to do her *homework*.

honest ('ɑnɪst) *adj.* 誠實的

You need to be *honest* with yourself.

honesty ('ɑnɪstɪ) *n.* 誠實

Honesty is the best policy.

honey ('hʌnɪ) *n.* 蜂蜜

Bees make *honey*.

Hong Kong ('hɑŋ'kɑŋ) *n.* 香港

Many people like to go shopping in *Hong Kong*.

hop (hɑp) *v.* 跳

The children are *hopping* on the bed.

hope (hop) *v.* 希望

I *hope* I will pass the exam.

horrible ('hɔrəbḷ , 'harəbḷ) *adj.* 可怕的
The food at the school was *horrible*.

horse (hɔrs) *n.* 馬
John rides a *horse* every morning.

hospital ('hɑspɪtḷ) *n.* 醫院
Doctors and nurses work in a *hospital*.

host (host) *n.* 主人
He was the *host* at the party.

hot (hɑt) *adj.* 熱的
It's very *hot* to stand in the sun.

hot dog *n.* 熱狗
I love to eat *hot dogs* while watching TV.

hotel (ho'tɛl) *n.* 旅館
He stayed in a *hotel* while he was in Spain.

hour (aʊr) *n.* 小時
I'll arrive at the station within an *hour*.

house (haʊs) *n.* 房子
Tom is going to buy a new *house*.

housewife ('haʊsˌwaɪf) *n.* 家庭主婦
My mother is a *housewife*.

housework ('haʊsˌwɜk) *n.* 家事
My brother and I shared the *housework*.

how (haʊ) *adv.* 如何
Her mother teaches her *how* to make a dress.

however (haʊˈɛvə) *adv.* 然而
This, *however*, is not your fault.

Hualian *n.* 花蓮
Hualian is the most beautiful place in Taiwan.

huge (hjudʒ) *adj.* 巨大的
There is a *huge* rock on the road.

human ('hjumən) *n.* 人
Wolves won't usually attack *humans*.

humble ('hʌmbl̩) *adj.* 謙卑的
Many famous people are very *humble*.

humid ('hjumɪd) *adj.* 潮濕的
It will be *humid* tomorrow.

humor ('hjumɚ) *n.* 幽默
(= *humour* 【英式用法】)
I don't see the *humor* of it.

humorous ('hjumərəs) *adj.* 幽默的
Those are *humorous* stories.

hundred ('hʌndrəd) *n.* 百
The number after ninety-nine is one *hundred*.

hunger ('hʌŋgɚ) *n.* 飢餓
He died of *hunger*.

hungry ('hʌŋgrɪ) *adj.* 飢餓的
I'm *hungry* and I need to eat.

hunt (hʌnt) *v.* 打獵
The hunters are *hunting* rabbits.

hunter ('hʌntɚ) *n.* 獵人
My father used to be a *hunter*.

hurry ('hɝɪ) *v.* 匆忙
He *hurried* home to tell his mother the news.

hurt (hɝt) *v.* 傷害
My back was *hurt* in the accident.

husband 〔'hʌzbənd 〕 *n.* 丈夫
Her *husband* has been working in France.

I i

I 〔 aɪ 〕 *pron.* 我
Am *I* right?

ice 〔 aɪs 〕 *n.* 冰
Nancy puts some *ice* in the drink.

ice cream *n.* 冰淇淋
Julia likes chocolate *ice cream*.

idea 〔 aɪ'diə 〕 *n.* 想法；點子
We should have a good *idea*.

if 〔 ɪf 〕 *conj.* 如果
If it rains, we won't go out.

ignore 〔 ɪg'nor 〕 *v.* 忽視
He *ignored* the traffic light and caused an accident.

ill 〔 ɪl 〕 *adj.* 生病的
Greg couldn't go to school because he was *ill*.

image ('ɪmɪdʒ) *n.* 形象

His behavior ruined his public *image*.

imagine (ɪ'mædʒɪn) *v.* 想像

You can *imagine* how nice the new car is.

impolite (͵ɪmpə'laɪt) *adj.* 無禮的

It was *impolite* of you not to answer the question.

import (ɪm'port) *v.* 進口

Europe *imports* coal from America.

importance (ɪm'portn̩s) *n.* 重要性

The *importance* of using your time well is quite clear.

important (ɪm'portn̩t) *adj.* 重要的

It is *important* to study English.

impossible (ɪm'pasəbl̩) *adj.* 不可能的

It's *impossible* for a cat to fly.

improve (ɪm'pruv) *v.* 改善

His grades are *improving*.

in 〔 ɪn 〕 *prep.* 在…之中

He lives *in* an apartment.

inch 〔 ɪntʃ 〕 *n.* 英吋

She is three *inches* taller than me.

include 〔 ɪn'klud 〕 *v.* 包括

The price *includes* the service charge.

including 〔 ɪn'kludɪŋ 〕 *prep.* 包括

I have to prepare food for seven people *including* me.

income 〔'ɪn,kʌm 〕 *n.* 收入

She has an *income* of 2,000 dollars a week.

increase 〔 ɪn'kris 〕 *v.* 增加

My weight has *increased* by ten pounds.

independent 〔,ɪndɪ'pɛndənt 〕 *adj.* 獨立的

He is *independent* of his parents.

indicate 〔'ɪndə,ket 〕 *v.* 指出

He *indicated* the fire station on the map for me.

individual (͵ɪndə'vɪdʒʊəl) *adj.* 個別的
n. 個人
We use *individual* towels.

industry ('ɪndəstrɪ) *n.* 工業
The automobile *industry* is thriving in Japan.

influence ('ɪnflʊəns) *n.* 影響
He had a great *influence* on those around him.

information (͵ɪnfə'meʃən) *n.* 資訊
You can get lots of *information* on the Internet.

injury ('ɪndʒərɪ) *n.* 傷害
He tried to prevent *injury* to the crops.

ink (ɪŋk) *n.* 墨水
My pen is running out of *ink*.

insect ('ɪnsɛkt) *n.* 昆蟲
A butterfly is an *insect*.

inside ('ɪn'saɪd) *prep.* 在…裡面
No one is *inside* the school.

insist (ɪn'sɪst) *v.* 堅持
My dad *insisted* that I go home for dinner
tonight.

inspire 〔 ɪnˈspaɪr 〕 v. 激勵
His brother *inspired* him to try one more time.

instance 〔ˈɪnstəns 〕 n. 實例
He cited many *instances*.

instant 〔ˈɪnstənt 〕 adj. 立即的
The country has a need for *instant* help.

instrument 〔ˈɪnstrəmənt 〕 n. 樂器
A guitar is a musical *instrument*.

intelligent 〔 ɪnˈtɛlədʒənt 〕 adj. 聰明的
Dogs are more *intelligent* than cats.

interest 〔ˈɪntrɪst 〕 v. 使感興趣
The story didn't *interest* me.

interested 〔ˈɪntrɪstɪd 〕 adj. 感興趣的
Peter is *interested* in airplanes.

interesting 〔ˈɪntrɪstɪŋ 〕 adj. 有趣的
The film is *interesting*.

international 〔ˌɪntəˈnæʃənḷ 〕 adj. 國際的
English is an *international* language.

Internet ('ɪntə̩nɛt) *n.* 網際網路
If you have a computer, you can use the
Internet to find information.

interrupt (͵ɪntə'rʌpt) *v.* 打斷
I don't want to be *interrupted*.

interview ('ɪntə̩vju) *v.* 面談；面試
He was *interviewed* for a management job.

into ('ɪntu) *prep.* 到…之內
I put some fruit *into* the refrigerator.

introduce (͵ɪntrə'djus) *v.* 介紹
The teacher *introduced* Ted to the class.

invent (ɪn'vɛnt) *v.* 發明
He *invented* the first electric clock.

investigate (ɪn'vɛstə̩get) *v.* 調查
We are *investigating* the cause of the accident.

invitation (͵ɪnvə'teʃən) *n.* 邀請
She received an *invitation* to the party.

invite (ɪn'vaɪt) *v.* 邀請
I *invited* her to dinner.

iron (ˈaɪɚn) *n.* 鐵

This gun is made of *iron*.

is (ɪz) *v.* be 的第三人稱單數

Paul *is* 14 years old.

island (ˈaɪlənd) *n.* 島

An *island* is a piece of land with water all around it.

it (ɪt) *pron.* 它;牠

I bought this knife yesterday and *it* cuts very well.

item (ˈaɪtəm) *n.* 項目

We have many *items* to discuss today.

its (ɪts) *pron.* it 的所有格

This chair has lost one of *its* legs.

itself (ɪtˈsɛlf) *pron.* it 的反身代名詞

The monkey saw *itself* in the water.

J j

jacket (ˈdʒækɪt) *n.* 夾克

The waiter in the white *jacket* is very polite.

jam 〔 dʒæm 〕 *n.* 果醬；阻塞
Cathy loves toast with strawberry *jam*.
I got caught in a traffic *jam*.

January 〔'dʒænjʊ‚ɛrɪ 〕 *n.* 一月
January is the first month of the year.

Japan 〔 dʒə'pæn 〕 *n.* 日本
There are four islands in *Japan*.

Japanese 〔‚dʒæpə'niz 〕 *adj.* 日本的
Many people are interested in *Japanese* culture.

jazz 〔 dʒæz 〕 *n.* 爵士樂
I like to listen to *jazz*.

jealous 〔'dʒɛləs 〕 *adj.* 嫉妒的
Mrs. Rudee is a *jealous* woman.

jeans 〔 dʒinz 〕 *n.pl.* 牛仔褲
Most teenagers like to wear *jeans*.

jeep 〔 dʒip 〕 *n.* 吉普車
A *jeep* is good as a family car.

job 〔 dʒɑb 〕 *n.* 工作
Kelly's *job* is to teach students math.

jog 〔 dʒɑg 〕 *v.* 慢跑

I like to *jog* in the morning.

join 〔 dʒɔɪn 〕 *v.* 加入

Scott *joined* the army last year.

joint 〔 dʒɔɪnt 〕 *n.* 關節

I have a pain in the knee *joint*.

joke 〔 dʒok 〕 *n.* 笑話

Mr. Black told a *joke* to his children.

journalist 〔 'dʒɝnḷɪst 〕 *n.* 記者

Stuart wants to be a *journalist*.

joy 〔 dʒɔɪ 〕 *n.* 喜悅

Our hearts fill with *joy* during Christmastime.

judge 〔 dʒʌdʒ 〕 *v.* 判斷   *n.* 法官

You can't *judge* a person by his appearance.
The *judge* sent the man to prison for a year.

juice 〔 dʒus 〕 *n.* 果汁

I drink a glass of orange *juice* every morning.

July 〔 dʒu'laɪ 〕 *n.* 七月

Helen is going to visit her aunt in *July*.

jump 〔 dʒʌmp 〕 *v.* 跳

That big dog *jumped* over the fence.

June 〔 dʒun 〕 *n.* 六月

June is the sixth month of the year.

junior high school *n.* 國中

I am studying in *junior high school*.

just 〔 dʒʌst 〕 *adv.* 只是；剛剛

My sister is *just* four years old, so she doesn't go to school.

K k

kangaroo 〔 ͺkæŋgəˈru 〕 *n.* 袋鼠

The *kangaroo* is a symbol of Australia.

Kaohsiung 〔 ˈgaʊˈʃjʊŋ 〕 *n.* 高雄

My brother is studying in *Kaohsiung*.

keep 〔 kip 〕 *v.* 保存

This book will be *kept* in the library.

ketchup 〔 ˈkɛtʃəp 〕 *n.* 蕃茄醬

Please pass me the *ketchup*.

key 〔 ki 〕 *n.* 鑰匙；關鍵 *adj.* 重要的

Do not lose the house *key*.

He has a *key* position in the department.

kick 〔 kɪk 〕 *v.* 踢

The children *kicked* the ball for fun.

kid 〔 kɪd 〕 *n.* 小孩

They've got three *kids*.

kill 〔 kɪl 〕 *v.* 殺死

Lions *kill* small animals for food.

kilogram 〔'kɪlə,græm 〕 *n.* 公斤（= *kg*）

We measure weight in *kilograms*.

kilometer 〔'kɪlə,mitɚ 〕 *n.* 公里

（= *km* = *kilometre* 【英式用法】）

Kaohsiung is about 400 *kilometers* away
from Taipei.

kind 〔 kaɪnd 〕 *n.* 種類 *adj.* 仁慈的

There are many *kinds* of fruit.

It's very *kind* of you.

kindergarten (ˈkɪndəˌgɑrtn̩) *n.* 幼稚園
My younger sister is studying in the
kindergarten.

king (kɪŋ) *n.* 國王
They made him *King* of England.

kingdom (ˈkɪŋdəm) *n.* 王國
Holland is a *kingdom*.

kiss (kɪs) *v.* 親吻
She *kissed* the baby on the face.

kitchen (ˈkɪtʃɪn) *n.* 廚房
Mary learned to cook in the *kitchen*.

kite (kaɪt) *n.* 風箏
Peter has never learned to fly a *kite*.

kitten (ˈkɪtn̩) *n.* 小貓 (= *kitty*)
A cat's baby is called a *kitten*.

kitty (ˈkɪtɪ) *n.* 小貓
Kitties are young cats.

knee 〔 ni 〕 *n.* 膝蓋
Tony fell and hurt his *knees*.

knife 〔 naɪf 〕 *n.* 刀子
Michelle used a *knife* to cut the apple.

knock 〔 nɑk 〕 *v.* 敲
The kid *knocked* on the door.

know 〔 no 〕 *v.* 知道
My mother *knows* a lot about animals.

knowledge 〔 ˈnɑlɪdʒ 〕 *n.* 知識
Knowledge is power.

koala 〔 kəˈɑlə 〕 *n.* 無尾熊
There are four *koalas* in the zoo.

Korea 〔 koˈriə 〕 *n.* 韓國
The weather in *Korea* is really cold.

Korean 〔 koˈriən 〕 *adj.* 韓國的
Do you like to eat *Korean* pickles?

KTV KTV
Zoe likes to go to a *KTV* with her friends.

L l

lack (læk) *v.* 缺乏
I don't seem to *lack* anything.

lady ('ledɪ) *n.* 女士
The young *lady* is very beautiful.

lake (lek) *n.* 湖
Jim lives near a *lake*.

lamb (læm) *n.* 小羊
A *lamb* is a young sheep.

lamp (læmp) *n.* 燈
Turn on the *lamp*, please.

land (lænd) *n.* 陸地
He traveled over *land* and sea.

language ('læŋgwɪdʒ) *n.* 語言
He can speak five *languages*.

lantern ('læntən) *n.* 燈籠
Streets are decorated with lamps during the
Lantern Festival.

Lantern Festival *n.* 元宵節
Many children are looking forward to the
Lantern Festival.

large 〔 lɑrdʒ 〕 *adj.* 大的
We are a big family so we need a *large* house.

last 〔 læst 〕 *adj.* 最後的
Charles came in *last* in the race.

late 〔 let 〕 *adv.* 遲到；晚
Jimmy comes to school *late* every day.

later 〔'letɚ〕 *adv.* 以後
I'll tell you *later*.

latest 〔'letɪst 〕 *adj.* 最新的
You can go to a KTV to sing the *latest* songs.

latter 〔'lætɚ 〕 *n.* 後者
I can speak English and Chinese, and the
latter is my mother tongue.

laugh 〔 læf 〕 *v.* 笑
Everybody *laughs* at him because he looks
funny.

law 〔 lɔ 〕 *n.* 法律

There is a *law* to stop people from driving too fast.

lawyer 〔'lɔjɚ 〕 *n.* 律師

His father is a *lawyer*.

lay 〔 le 〕 *v.* 放置

Judy *laid* the pencils on the desk.

lazy 〔'lezɪ 〕 *adj.* 懶惰的

My brother is very *lazy*.

lead 〔 lid 〕 *v.* 帶領

The teacher *leads* students to the playground.

leader 〔'lidɚ 〕 *n.* 領導者

We chose Diane to be our class *leader*.

leadership 〔'lidɚʃɪp 〕 *n.* 領導（地位）

We are under the *leadership* of Samuel.

leaf 〔 lif 〕 *n.* 葉子

It's fall, and the *leaves* on the trees are falling.

learn 〔 lɜn 〕 *v.* 學習

I'm going to *learn* French.

least ﹝ list ﹞ *adj.* 最少的

He has the *least* experience of them all.

leave ﹝ liv ﹞ *v.* 離開

The bus will *leave* the station in ten minutes.

left ﹝ lɛft ﹞ *v.* leave 的過去式 *adj.* 左邊的

Mike's wife *left* him last year.

He likes to write with his *left* hand.

leg ﹝ lɛg ﹞ *n.* 腿

A dog has four *legs*.

legal ﹝'ligl﹞ *adj.* 合法的

He is the *legal* successor to the king.

lemon ﹝'lɛmən﹞ *n.* 檸檬

A *lemon* is a fruit with a very sour taste.

lend ﹝ lɛnd ﹞ *v.* 借 (出)

Can you *lend* me your car?

length ﹝ lɛŋθ ﹞ *n.* 長度

The river has a *length* of 100 kilometers.

less ﹝ lɛs ﹞ *adv.* 較少地

A radio costs *less* than a television.

lesson (ˈlɛsn̩) *n.* 課
Anna took a piano *lesson*.

let (lɛt) *v.* 讓
My father won't *let* me go to the concert.

letter (ˈlɛtɚ) *n.* 信；字母
Mary has written a *letter* to her friend.

lettuce (ˈlɛtɪs) *n.* 萵苣
Lettuce is a plant with large green leaves.

level (ˈlɛvl̩) *n.* 水準；程度
Robert is a man with a high *level* of
education.

library (ˈlaɪˌbrɛrɪ) *n.* 圖書館
Don't make a loud noise in the *library*.

lick (lɪk) *v.* 舔
Many pets like to *lick* their owners to show
their love.

lid (lɪd) *n.* 蓋子
Take the *lid* off the pot.

lie 〔 laɪ 〕 v. 說謊　v. 躺
My aunt *lies* about her age.
He went to *lie* down on the bed.

life 〔 laɪf 〕 n. 生命；生活
Life is full of surprises.

lift 〔 lɪft 〕 v. 舉起
The mother *lifts* her baby up gently.

light 〔 laɪt 〕 n. 光　adj. 輕的
We cannot see without *light*.
This box is *light* to carry.

lightning 〔'laɪtnɪŋ 〕 n. 閃電
During the storm, we saw *lightning* in the sky.

like 〔 laɪk 〕 v. 喜歡　prep. 像…
I don't *like* pop music.
There is no place *like* home.

likely 〔'laɪklɪ 〕 adj. 可能的
It is *likely* to rain soon.

limit 〔'lɪmɪt 〕 v. 限制
Limit your answer to yes or no.

line 〔 laɪn 〕 *n.* 線
Draw a *line* down the center of that page.

link 〔 lɪŋk 〕 *v.* 連結
The new canal will *link* the two rivers.

lion 〔 'laɪən 〕 *n.* 獅子
Lions are wild animals that look like big cats.

lip 〔 lɪp 〕 *n.* 嘴唇
We move our *lips* when we speak.

liquid 〔 'lɪkwɪd 〕 *n.* 液體
Oil, milk and water are all *liquids*.

list 〔 lɪst 〕 *n.* 名單
There were ten names on the *list*.

listen 〔 'lɪsn̩ 〕 *v.* 聽
Carol likes to *listen* to the radio.

liter 〔 'litɚ 〕 *n.* 公升
He drank a *liter* of milk.

litter 〔 'lɪtɚ 〕 *v.* 亂丟垃圾
The sign said, "No *littering* in the park."

little (ˈlɪtḷ) *adj.* 小的;少的

Your *little* sister is so cute.

live (lɪv) *v.* 住

He still *lives* with his parents.

living room *n.* 客廳

My father is watching TV in the *living room*.

loaf (lof) *n.* 一條麵包

My mother puts a *loaf* in the basket.

local (ˈlokḷ) *adj.* 當地的

I'm not used to the *local* customs yet.

lock (lɑk) *v.* 鎖

Don't forget to *lock* the door.

London (ˈlʌndən) *n.* 倫敦

London is the capital of England.

locker (ˈlɑkɚ) *n.* 置物櫃

There is a book in the *locker*.

lonely (ˈlonlɪ) *adj.* 寂寞的

Jimmy is a *lonely* boy.

long ﹝ lɔŋ ﹞ *adj.* 長的
My hair is *long*.

look ﹝ lʊk ﹞ *v.* 看
I'm *looking* at a small dog.

lose ﹝ luz ﹞ *v.* 遺失
Nancy *loses* her pens very often.

loser ﹝ 'luzɚ ﹞ *n.* 失敗者
He is not a bad *loser*; he takes defeat well.

loss ﹝ lɔs ﹞ *n.* 損失
It's a great *loss* to me.

lot ﹝ lɑt ﹞ *n.* 許多
We always have a *lot* of rain in May.

loud ﹝ laʊd ﹞ *adj.* 大聲的
The man speaks in a *loud* voice.

love ﹝ lʌv ﹞ *v.* 愛
If you *love* someone, you'll feel happy.

lovely ﹝ 'lʌvlɪ ﹞ *adj.* 可愛的
Sara is a *lovely* girl.

lover 〔'lʌvɚ〕 *n.* 愛人

Ken's *lover* died last year.

low 〔 lo 〕 *adj.* 低的

This chair is too *low* for Rose.

lucky 〔'lʌkɪ〕 *adj.* 幸運的

You are a *lucky* girl to have so many good friends.

lunch 〔 lʌntʃ 〕 *n.* 午餐

We had *lunch* at one o'clock.

M m

ma'am 〔 mæm 〕 *n.* 夫人

Yes, *ma'am*?

machine 〔 məˈʃin 〕 *n.* 機器

Machines help us to do things more easily.

mad 〔 mæd 〕 *adj.* 發瘋的

He behaves as if he were *mad*.

magazine 〔͵mægəˈzin 〕 *n.* 雜誌

Children's *magazines* are full of interesting pictures.

magic ('mædʒɪk) *n.* 魔法;魔術
The girl was turned by *magic* into a swan.

magician (mə'dʒɪʃən) *n.* 魔術師
A *magician* can do strange tricks to surprise
people.

mail (mel) *n.* 郵件
My friend contacted me by *mail*.

mailman ('mel,mæn) *n.* 郵差
(= *mail carrier* = *postman*【英式用法】)
The *mailman* came late today.

main (men) *adj.* 主要的
This is the *main* building of our college.

maintain (men'ten) *v.* 維持
The increase in sales is being *maintained*.

major ('medʒə) *adj.* 主要的;重要的 *v.* 主修
Li Po was a *major* poet in China.
He *majored* in history.

make (mek) *v.* 製造
Don't *make* loud noises.

male 〔 mel 〕 *n.* 男性
Boys are *males* and girls are females.

mall 〔 mɔl 〕 *n.* 購物中心
I'm on my way to the *mall*.

man 〔 mæn 〕 *n.* 男人
He is a very good-looking *man*.

manager 〔'mænɪdʒɚ 〕 *n.* 經理
His father is a good *manager*.

Mandarin 〔'mændərɪn 〕 *n.* 國語
My grandmother can't speak *Mandarin*.

mango 〔'mæŋgo 〕 *n.* 芒果
Mangoes are my favorite fruit.

manner 〔'mænɚ 〕 *n.* 態度；(*pl.*) 禮貌
Susan smiled in a friendly *manner*.
He has no *manners*.

many 〔'mɛnɪ 〕 *adj.* 很多的
There are *many* rooms in the hotel.

map 〔 mæp 〕 *n.* 地圖
Have you got the *map* of Paris?

March 〔 mɑrtʃ 〕 *n.* 三月 (= *Mar.*)
March is the third month of the year.

mark 〔 mɑrk 〕 *n.* 分數
The teacher gave me good *marks* for my report.

marker 〔'mɑrkɚ 〕 *n.* 記分員;做記號的工具
Pat is a very strict *marker*.

market 〔'mɑrkɪt 〕 *n.* 市場
She sold vegetables in the *market*.

marriage 〔'mærɪdʒ 〕 *n.* 婚姻
Her first *marriage* was not very happy.

married 〔'mærɪd 〕 *adj.* 結婚的
Is she *married*?

marry 〔'mærɪ 〕 *v.* 和…結婚
Bill asked Grace to *marry* him.

marvelous 〔'mɑrvḷəs 〕 *adj.* 神奇的;很棒的
(= *marvellous* 【英式用法】)
Have you ever seen such a *marvelous* movie?

mask 〔 mæsk 〕 *n.* 面具

Tom has to wear a *mask* in the school play.

mass 〔 mæs 〕 *n.* 團；大量

I see a large *mass* of clouds.

master 〔'mæstɚ 〕 *v.* 精通

He has *mastered* a lot of languages.

mat 〔 mæt 〕 *n.* 墊子

The *mat* is the same size as this room.

match 〔 mætʃ 〕 *v.* 和…相配

This tie doesn't *match* your suit.

material 〔 mə'tɪrɪəl 〕 *n.* 材料

Plastic is a widely used *material*.

math 〔 mæθ 〕 *n.* 數學 (= *mathematics*)

They were doing *math* exercises when I left.

matter 〔'mætɚ 〕 *n.* 事情   *v.* 重要；要緊

That's another *matter*.

It doesn't *matter* to me if I miss my train.

maximum 〔'mæksəməm 〕 *n.* 最大量

She types a *maximum* of seventy words per minute.

May 〔 me 〕 *n.* 五月
May is the fifth month of the year.

may 〔 me 〕 *aux.* 可以
You *may* go if you want.

maybe 〔'mebɪ 〕 *adv.* 或許
Maybe my mother will come here next month.

me 〔 mi 〕 *pron.* I 的受格
He doesn't know *me*.

meal 〔 mil 〕 *n.* 一餐
Breakfast is our morning *meal*.

mean 〔 min 〕 *v.* 意思是
What do you *mean*?

meaning 〔'minɪŋ 〕 *n.* 意思
I don't know the *meaning* of the word.

means 〔 minz 〕 *n.* 方法
Do you know of any *means* to get there?

measure 〔'mɛʒɚ 〕 *v.* 測量
The man tried to *measure* the floor.

meat 〔 mit 〕 *n.* 肉

Pork is a popular kind of *meat*.

mechanic 〔 mə'kænɪk 〕 *n.* 技工

Mr. Brown is a good *mechanic*.

media 〔'midɪə 〕 *n. pl.* 媒體

You can know the news through the mass *media*.

medicine 〔'mɛdəsn̩ 〕 *n.* 藥

The doctor treated me by using *medicine*.

medium 〔'midɪəm 〕 *adj.* 中等的   *n.* 媒體；
媒介（複數形為 mediums 或 media）

The man is of *medium* height.
The newspaper is a prime *medium* of communication.

meet 〔 mit 〕 *v.* 和…見面

I will *meet* you at the library.

meeting 〔'mitɪŋ 〕 *n.* 會議

Ralph will have an important *meeting* tomorrow.

melon (ˈmɛlən) *n.* 甜瓜
Would you like a slice of *melon*?

member (ˈmɛmbɚ) *n.* 成員
Jack is a *member* of a football team.

memory (ˈmɛmərɪ) *n.* 記憶
I have no *memory* of my mother.

men's room *n.* 男廁
Where is the *men's room*?

menu (ˈmɛnju) *n.* 菜單
Let us see what's on the *menu* today.

message (ˈmɛsɪdʒ) *n.* 訊息
He sent me a *message* by mail.

metal (ˈmɛtl̩) *n.* 金屬
Iron, gold and silver are *metals*.

meter (ˈmitɚ) *n.* 公尺 (= m = metre【英式用法】)
We measure length in *meters*.

method (ˈmɛθəd) *n.* 方法
I want to know a good *method* for learning
English.

microwave ﹝'maɪkrəˌwev﹞ *n.* 微波
I bought a new *microwave* oven for my mother.

middle ﹝'mɪdl̩﹞ *n.* 中間
He was born in the *middle* of April.

midnight ﹝'mɪdˌnaɪt﹞ *n.* 半夜
Our party ended at *midnight*.

might ﹝maɪt﹞ *aux.* may 的過去式
He *might* not be back until tonight.

mile ﹝maɪl﹞ *n.* 英哩
Wendy walks two *miles* to school every day.

military ﹝'mɪləˌtɛrɪ﹞ *adj.* 軍事的
Henry plans to attend a *military* academy.

milk ﹝mɪlk﹞ *n.* 牛奶
Mary drinks a glass of *milk* every morning.

milk shake *n.* 奶昔
Edward treated me to a *milk shake*.

million ﹝'mɪljən﹞ *n.* 百萬
He made a *million* dollars.

mind〔maɪnd〕*n.* 心   *v.* 介意

You are always on my *mind*.

Do you *mind* if I put my bag here?

mine〔maɪn〕*pron.* I 的所有格代名詞

That wasn't his fault; it was *mine*.

minor〔'maɪnə〕*adj.* 較小的；不嚴重的

v. 輔修

He got a *minor* injury.

Maria *minored* in biology in college.

minus〔'maɪnəs〕*prep.* 減

One *minus* one is zero.

minute〔'mɪnɪt〕*n.* 分鐘

An hour has sixty *minutes*.

mirror〔'mɪrə〕*n.* 鏡子

The *mirror* reflects your face.

Miss〔mɪs〕*n.* 小姐

Miss Daisy called you last night.

miss〔mɪs〕*v.* 錯過；想念

John *missed* the train to Tainan.

missing ﹝'mɪsɪŋ﹞ *adj.* 缺少的；找不到的
There are three pages *missing* in this book.

mistake ﹝mə'stek﹞ *n.* 錯誤
Jill has made a *mistake*.

mix ﹝mɪks﹞ *v.* 混合
Helen *mixes* flour, eggs and sugar to bake a cake.

model ﹝'mɑdl﹞ *n.* 模型
He made a *model* of his new house.

modern ﹝'mɑdən﹞ *adj.* 現代的
There are a lot of *modern* buildings in New York.

moment ﹝'momənt﹞ *n.* 片刻
I fell asleep for a *moment*.

Monday ﹝'mʌndɪ﹞ *n.* 星期一 (= *Mon.*)
Monday is the day after Sunday.

money ﹝'mʌnɪ﹞ *n.* 錢
People need *money* to live their lives.

monkey (ˈmʌŋkɪ) *n.* 猴子
Monkeys like to climb trees.

monster (ˈmɑnstɚ) *n.* 怪物
The film is about a *monster*.

month (mʌnθ) *n.* 月
She has been here for a *month*.

monthly (ˈmʌnθlɪ) *adj.* 每月的
I bought a *monthly* magazine yesterday.

moon (mun) *n.* 月亮
I love the light of a full *moon*.

mop (mɑp) *v.* 用拖把拖（地）
I *mopped* the floor every day.

more (mor) *adj.* 更多的
James needs *more* money to buy a new house.

morning (ˈmɔrnɪŋ) *n.* 早上
Kim always gets up early in the *morning*.

mosquito (məˈskito) *n.* 蚊子
Mosquitoes are small insects which can carry diseases.

most〔most〕 *adj.* 大多數的
Most people like Taiwanese food.

mother〔'mʌðɚ〕 *n.* 母親
(= *mom* = *mommy* = *momma* = *mama*)
She is a *mother* of three children.

Mother's Day *n.* 母親節
I helped my mother do housework on
Mother's Day.

motion〔'moʃən〕 *n.* 動作
All her *motions* were graceful.

motorcycle〔'motɚ͵saɪkḷ〕 *n.* 摩托車
(= *motorbike*【英式用法】)
There are more and more *motorcycles* on
the streets.

mountain〔'maʊntṇ〕 *n.* 山
Alex is walking to the top of the *mountain*.

mountain climbing〔'maʊntṇ'klaɪmɪŋ〕 *n.*
爬山
My father enjoys *mountain climbing*.

mouse〔maʊs〕 *n.* 老鼠
I like Mickey *Mouse* very much.

mouth ﹝maʊθ﹞ *n.* 嘴巴
His *mouth* is full of rice.

move ﹝muv﹞ *v.* 移動
She *moved* away from the window.

movement ﹝'muvmənt﹞ *n.* 動作
Watch the baby's *movements*.

movie ﹝'muvɪ﹞ *n.* 電影 (= *film* = *picture*)
I want to see a *movie* with her.

movie theater   *n.* 電影院
There is a *movie theater* near my house.

Mr. ﹝'mɪstə﹞ *n.* 先生 (= *Mr*)
Mr. White teaches us music.

Mrs. ﹝'mɪsɪz﹞ *n.* 太太 (= *Mrs*)
Mrs. Brown is our math teacher.

MRT   *n.* 捷運 (= *mass rapid transit* = *subway* = *underground* = *metro*)
I take the *MRT* to school every day.

Ms. 〔 mɪz 〕 *n.* 女士 (= Ms)

Ms. Smith is a lovely lady.

MTV 音樂電視節目 (= *Music Television*)

My sister likes to watch *MTV* very much.

much 〔 mʌtʃ 〕 *adj.* 許多的

Don't eat too *much* cake.

mud 〔 mʌd 〕 *n.* 泥巴

When it rains, the ground is covered with *mud*.

museum 〔 mju'ziəm 〕 *n.* 博物館

The students went to the history *museum*.

music 〔'mjuzɪk 〕 *n.* 音樂

Helen listened to *music* on the radio.

musician 〔 mju'zɪʃən 〕 *n.* 音樂家

A *musician* is a person who plays a musical instrument.

must 〔 mʌst 〕 *aux.* 必須

You *must* do your homework.

my 〔 maɪ 〕 *adj.* I 的所有格

Paul is *my* best friend.

myself 〔 maɪˈsɛlf 〕 *pron.* I 的反身代名詞
I've done this job by *myself*.

N n

nail 〔 nel 〕 *n.* 釘子
Henry put a *nail* in the wall to hang a picture.

name 〔 nem 〕 *n.* 名字
David is the *name* of the baby.

napkin 〔ˈnæpkɪn 〕 *n.* 餐巾
She handed him a *napkin*.

narrow 〔ˈnæro 〕 *adj.* 窄的
The road is very *narrow*.

nation 〔ˈneʃən 〕 *n.* 國家
There are many *nations* in the world.

national 〔ˈnæʃənḷ 〕 *adj.* 國家的
We should respect our *national* flag.

natural 〔ˈnætʃərəl 〕 *adj.* 自然的
I want to live a *natural* life.

nature〔'netʃɚ〕*n.* 大自然

The beauty of *nature* inspired many poets.

naughty〔'nɔtɪ〕*adj.* 頑皮的

These two brothers are really *naughty*.

near〔nɪr〕*prep.* 在…附近

My house is *near* the school.

nearly〔'nɪrlɪ〕*adv.* 幾乎

It's *nearly* lunchtime.

necessary〔'nɛsə,sɛrɪ〕*adj.* 必需的

Sleep is *necessary* for good health.

neck〔nɛk〕*n.* 脖子

She has a long *neck*.

necklace〔'nɛklɪs〕*n.* 項鍊

My friend gave me a *necklace* on my birthday.

need〔nid〕*v.* 需要

I *need* to know everything before making a decision.

needle〔'nidl̩〕*n.* 針

I need a *needle* to mend a hole in this dress.

negative (ˈnɛgətɪv) *adj.* 否定的

He gave a *negative* answer to my proposal.

neighbor (ˈnebɚ) *n.* 鄰居

(= *neighbour*【英式用法】)

I'm lucky to have you as my *neighbor*.

neither (ˈniðɚ) *adv.* 既不…（也不）

I love *neither* James nor his brother.

nephew (ˈnɛfju) *n.* 姪兒；外甥

My grandfather has two *nephews*.

nervous (ˈnɜvəs) *adj.* 緊張的

I always feel *nervous* just before having
an exam.

nest (nɛst) *n.* 巢

There are six birds in the *nest*.

never (ˈnɛvɚ) *adv.* 從未

She has *never* been to a nightclub.

new (nju) *adj.* 新的

I'm going to buy a *new* car next Friday.

news 〔 njuz 〕 *n.* 新聞
That man was on the *news* for killing someone.

newspaper 〔'njuz,pepɚ 〕 *n.* 報紙
I read *newspapers* every day to know what
is happening in the world.

New Year's Day *n.* 元旦
I want to have a party on *New Year's Day*.

New Year's Eve *n.* 除夕
What will you do on *New Year's Eve*?

New York 〔 nju'jɔrk 〕 *n.* 紐約
Tony's parents moved to *New York* ten years
ago.

next 〔 nɛkst 〕 *adj.* 下一個
Linda is the *next* person to give a speech.

nice 〔 naɪs 〕 *adj.* 好的
Julie is a very *nice* person.

nice-looking 〔'naɪs'lʊkɪŋ 〕 *adj.* 好看的
My boyfriend is a *nice-looking* guy.

niece〔 nis 〕*n.* 姪女；外甥女

Mrs. Black is going to visit her *niece*.

night 〔 naɪt 〕*n.* 晚上

My father hates to drive at *night*.

nine 〔 naɪn 〕*adj.* 九的

Her son is *nine* years old.

nineteen 〔'naɪn'tin 〕*adj.* 十九的

Leo will be *nineteen* tomorrow.

nineteenth 〔'naɪn'tinθ 〕*adj.* 第十九

Today is my *nineteenth* birthday.

ninety 〔'naɪntɪ 〕*n.* 九十

My grandpa died at the age of *ninety*.

ninth 〔 naɪnθ 〕*adj.* 第九

My birthday is on the *ninth* of September.

no 〔 no 〕*adv.* 不 (= *nope*)

No, I don't have a pencil.

nobody 〔'no,bɑdɪ 〕*pron.* 沒有人

There is *nobody* inside the room.

nod 〔 nɑd 〕 *v.* 點頭

She *nodded* to me on the street.

noise 〔 nɔɪz 〕 *n.* 噪音

I hate that *noise* because it drives me crazy.

noisy 〔'nɔɪzɪ 〕 *adj.* 吵鬧的

Don't be so *noisy*!

none 〔 nʌn 〕 *pron.* 無一人；無一物

None of us are Americans.

noodle 〔'nudḷ 〕 *n.* 麵

Chinese food is often served with rice or
noodles.

noon 〔 nun 〕 *n.* 正午

Lunch will be served at *noon*.

nor 〔 nɔr 〕 *conj.* 也不

He can neither read *nor* write.

north 〔 nɔrθ 〕 *n.* 北方

The wind is blowing from the *north*.

northern 〔'nɔrðən 〕 *adj.* 北方的

He likes to visit the *northern* states in America.

nose〔noz〕*n.* 鼻子
The clown has his *nose* painted red.

not〔nɑt〕*adv.* 不
Sally is *not* here today.

note〔not〕*n.* 筆記
She never takes *notes* in class.

notebook〔'not,bʊk〕*n.* 筆記本
I've written all the new words in my *notebook*.

nothing〔'nʌθɪŋ〕*pron.* 什麼也沒有
I have *nothing* if I have to live without you.

notice〔'notɪs〕*v.* 注意到 *n.* 告示
Did you *notice* her new dress?
There is a *notice* on the board.

novel〔'nɑvḷ〕*n.* 小說 *adj.* 新奇的
I like to read *novels* in my free time.
That idea is *novel* to me.

November〔no'vɛmbɚ〕*n.* 十一月（= *Nov.*）
Paul married Mary in *November*.

now〔naʊ〕*adv.* 現在
We should start working *now*.

number 〔'nʌmbɚ〕 *n.* 號碼

Each house has a *number*.

nurse 〔nɝs〕 *n.* 護士

A *nurse* is taking care of a patient.

nut 〔nʌt〕 *n.* 堅果

Henry likes to eat *nuts*.

O o

obey 〔ə'be〕 *v.* 服從

I didn't *obey* my parents when I was young.

object 〔'ɑbdʒɪkt〕 *n.* 物體 〔əb'dʒɛkt〕 *v.* 反對

I can see a shining *object* in the sky.

The boss wouldn't *object* if you smoked in his office.

occur 〔ə'kɝ〕 *v.* 發生

They say that the traffic accident *occurred* at midnight.

ocean 〔'oʃən〕 *n.* 海洋

Oceans are very deep seas.

o'clock 〔 əˈklɑk 〕 *adv.* …點鐘
It's now seven *o'clock*.

October 〔 ɑkˈtobə 〕 *n.* 十月 (= *Oct.*)
October comes after September.

of 〔 əv 〕 *prep.* …的
I know the end *of* the story.

off 〔 ɔf 〕 *prep.* 離開
I can't take my eyes *off* her.

offer 〔 ˈɔfə 〕 *v.* 提供
He *offered* me a better job.

office 〔 ˈɔfɪs 〕 *n.* 辦公室
Lucy works in an *office*.

officer 〔 ˈɔfəsə 〕 *n.* 警官
The police *officer* stopped the car.

official 〔 əˈfɪʃəl 〕 *adj.* 正式的
The statement is not *official*.

often 〔 ˈɔfən 〕 *adv.* 經常
I *often* go to the library at lunchtime.

oil 〔 ɔɪl 〕 *n.* 油
Pat puts *oil* in the pan to fry an egg.

OK 〔 'o'ke 〕 *adv.* 順利地；很好地
(= *O.K.* = *ok* = *o.k.*)
This car runs *OK*.

old 〔 old 〕 *adj.* 古老的
China is an *old* country.

omit 〔 o'mɪt 〕 *v.* 省略
Don't *omit* his name from the list.

on 〔 ɑn 〕 *prep.* 在…之上
The food is *on* the table.

once 〔 wʌns 〕 *adv.* 一次
Henry has been to Paris *once*.

one 〔 wʌn 〕 *adj.* 一個
Dolly has *one* cat and two dogs.

oneself 〔 wʌn'sɛlf 〕 *pron.* 自己
One should not praise *oneself*.

onion 〔 'ʌnjən 〕 *n.* 洋蔥
Do not put the *onion* in the soup.

only ('onlɪ) *adj.* 唯一的
The *only* thing I can't stand is cheating.

open ('opən) *v.* 打開
Ben *opened* his bag to take out the books.

operate ('ɑpə,ret) *v.* 運轉；操作
The machines will not *operate* properly.

operation (,ɑpə'reʃən) *n.* 手術
I had an *operation* on my heart.

opinion (ə'pɪnjən) *n.* 意見
Mary has no *opinion* at all.

opportunity (,ɑpə'tjunətɪ) *n.* 機會
I have no *opportunity* to make a trip.

or (ɔr) *conj.* 或
Either one *or* two is fine.

orange ('ɔrɪndʒ) *n.* 柳橙
Sarah bought some *oranges* at the supermarket.

order ('ɔrdə) *v.* 點 (餐)　　*n.* 命令
We *ordered* our dinner.
You have to learn to obey *orders*.

ordinary (ˈɔrdn̩ˌɛrɪ) *adj.* 普通的

We just want an *ordinary* lunch.

organization (ˌɔrgənəˈzeʃən) *n.* 組織

(= *organisation* 【英式用法】)

He was engaged in the *organization* of the
tennis club.

organize (ˈɔrgənˌaɪz) *v.* 組織

(= *organise* 【英式用法】)

They want to *organize* a political party.

other (ˈʌðɚ) *adj.* 其他的

I have many *other* things to do.

our (aʊr) *adj.* we 的所有格

We have to carry *our* books to school every day.

ours (aʊrz) *pron.* we 的所有代名詞

His house is larger than *ours*.

ourselves (aʊrˈsɛlvz) *pron.* we 的反身代名詞

We bought *ourselves* a new house.

out (aʊt) *adv.* 到外面

Jimmy went *out* to play.

outer space *n.* 外太空
There are many stars in *outer space*.

outside ('aʊt'saɪd) *adv.* 在外面
Many people who are *outside* wanted to get in.

oven ('ʌvən) *n.* 烤箱
The maid baked a chicken in the *oven*.

over ('ovɚ) *prep.* 越過
John can jump *over* that fence.

overpass ('ovɚ,pæs) *n.* 天橋
It's safe for pedestrians to use the *overpass*.

overseas ('ovɚ'siz) *adj.* 海外的
This is my first *overseas* trip.

overweight ('ovɚ'wet) *adj.* 過重的
My father is *overweight*.

own (on) *v.* 擁有
Who *owns* this land?

owner ('onɚ) *n.* 擁有者
She is the *owner* of the company.

ox 〔 ɑks 〕 *n.* 公牛
There is an *ox* over there.

P p

P.M. 〔'pi'ɛm 〕 *adv.* 下午 (= *p.m.* = *PM*)
It's 5:30 *P.M.*

pack 〔 pæk 〕 *v.* 包裝
All clothes will be *packed* into the bag.

package 〔'pækɪdʒ 〕 *n.* 包裹
Here is a *package* for you.

page 〔 pedʒ 〕 *n.* 頁
How many *pages* are there in this book?

pain 〔 pen 〕 *n.* 疼痛
She was in *pain* after she broke her leg.

painful 〔'penfəl 〕 *adj.* 痛苦的
I want to forget the *painful* experience.

paint 〔 pent 〕 *v.* 油漆
I *painted* my house blue.

painter (ˈpentɚ) *n.* 油漆工人

We need to hire two more *painters*.

painting (ˈpentɪŋ) *n.* 畫

That is an oil *painting*.

pair (pɛr) *n.* 一雙

Lucy forgot a *pair* of shoes at school.

pajamas (pəˈdʒɑməz) *n.pl.* 睡衣
(= *pyjamas*【英式用法】)

I bought a new pair of *pajamas* today.

pale (pel) *adj.* 蒼白的

She was *pale* with fear.

pan (pæn) *n.* 平底鍋

My aunt fried an egg in a *pan*.

panda (ˈpændə) *n.* 貓熊

We can see *pandas* in China.

pants (pænts) *n.pl.* 褲子
(= *trousers* (ˈtraʊzɚz)【英式用法】)

I saw him in a white shirt and black *pants*.

papaya 〔 pə'pajə 〕 *n.* 木瓜

Rose bought a *papaya* at the market.

paper 〔'pepɚ〕 *n.* 紙

This doll is made of *paper*.

pardon 〔'pɑrdn̩〕 *n.* 原諒

I beg your *pardon*.

parents 〔'pɛrənts〕 *n. pl.* 父母

Linda stays with her *parents*.

Paris 〔'pærɪs〕 *n.* 巴黎

Susan took a lot of beautiful pictures in *Paris*.

park 〔 pɑrk 〕 *v.* 停（車）   *n.* 公園

She *parked* her car there for five minutes.

I like to take a walk in the *park* after dinner.

parking lot   *n.* 停車場

I'm looking for the *parking lot*.

parrot 〔'pærət〕 *n.* 鸚鵡

Parrots are birds of very bright colors.

part 〔 pɑrt 〕 *n.* 部分

A leg is a *part* of the body.

particular (pɚˈtɪkjələ) *adj.* 特別的
I have nothing *particular* to do today.

partner (ˈpɑrtnɚ) *n.* 夥伴
They were *partners* in business.

party (ˈpɑrtɪ) *n.* 宴會
Jimmy is going to have a birthday *party*.

pass (pæs) *v.* 通過
Tommy wants to *pass* this exam.

passenger (ˈpæsn̩dʒɚ) *n.* 乘客
The bus can carry fifty *passengers*.

past (pæst) *prep.* 經過
To get to the park, you have to walk *past* the
bank.

paste (pest) *v.* 黏貼
Patrick *pasted* pictures of animals in his
book.

path (pæθ) *n.* 小路
Harry likes to walk down this *path* to get to
the lake.

patient ('peʃənt) *n.* 病人　*adj.* 有耐心的
There are many *patients* in the hospital.
He is a very *patient* man.

pattern ('pætən) *n.* 樣式；圖案
Designers have many dress *patterns*.

pause (pɔz) *n.* 暫停
After a short *pause*, Lori kept on working.

pay (pe) *v.* 付錢
I'll *pay* for the meal.

PE ('pi'i) *n.* 體育 (= *physical education*)
We have a *PE* class today.

peace (pis) *n.* 和平
Both warring nations longed for *peace*.

peaceful ('pisfəl) *adj.* 平靜的
The couple leads a *peaceful* life.

peach (pitʃ) *n.* 桃子
Peaches are my favorite fruit.

pear (pɛr) *n.* 梨子
A *pear* is a sweet and juicy fruit.

pen 〔 pɛn 〕 *n.* 筆
Could you lend me a *pen*, please?

pencil 〔'pɛnsḷ 〕 *n.* 鉛筆
Paul signs his name in *pencil*.

pencil box *n.* 鉛筆盒 (= *pencil case*)
Tom collects many kinds of *pencil boxes*.

people 〔'pipḷ 〕 *n.pl.* 人
Many *people* ride the MRT at rush hour.

pepper 〔'pɛpɚ 〕 *n.* 胡椒
I put *pepper* on the pizza.

perfect 〔'pɝfɪkt 〕 *adj.* 完美的
Emily's schoolwork is *perfect*.

perhaps 〔 pɚ'hæps 〕 *adv.* 或許
Perhaps your book is on your desk.

period 〔'pɪrɪəd 〕 *n.* 期間；時期
This was the most difficult *period* of his life.

person 〔'pɝsṇ 〕 *n.* 人
There are three *persons* in the living room.

personal (´pɜsn̩l) *adj.* 個人的
Martin received a *personal* letter.

pet (pɛt) *n.* 寵物
Mike keeps a lot of *pets*.

Philippines (´fɪlə‚pinz) *n.* 菲律賓
There are many islands in *Philippines*.

phone (fon) *n.* 電話 (= *telephone*)
Please answer the *phone*.

photo (´foto) *n.* 照片 (= *photograph*)
I took a lot of *photo*s on my trip.

photograph (´fotə‚græf) *n.* 照片 (= *photo*)
This is my girlfriend's *photograph*.

photographer (fə´tɑgrəfɚ) *n.* 攝影師
He is a great *photographer*.

physics (´fɪzɪks) *n.* 物理學
Physics is my favorite subject.

piano (pɪ´æno) *n.* 鋼琴
Lucy played the *piano* in the concert.

pick ﹝ pɪk ﹞ v. 挑選
Frank *picked* a ball from the box.

picnic ﹝'pɪknɪk ﹞ n. 野餐
Our family enjoyed a *picnic* on Sunday.

picture ﹝'pɪktʃɚ ﹞ n. 圖畫
An artist is painting a *picture*.

pie ﹝ paɪ ﹞ n. 派
Elsa made a cherry *pie* by herself.

piece ﹝ pis ﹞ n. 一張
I gave him a *piece* of paper.

pig ﹝ pɪg ﹞ n. 豬
The farmer raises *pigs*.

pigeon ﹝'pɪdʒɪn ﹞ n. 鴿子
A *pigeon* lives on the roof of my house.

pile ﹝ paɪl ﹞ n. 堆
He puts the fruit in *piles* under the tree.

pillow ﹝'pɪlo ﹞ n. 枕頭
This *pillow* is so hard that I can't sleep.

pin 〔 pɪn 〕 *n.* 大頭針
Lisa used *pins* to hold pieces of cloth together.

pineapple 〔'paɪnˌæpl̩ 〕 *n.* 鳳梨
A *pineapple* has a sweet taste.

pink 〔 pɪŋk 〕 *n.* 粉紅色
The lady wore *pink* at the party.

pipe 〔 paɪp 〕 *n.* 煙斗
I handed my father a *pipe*.

pizza 〔'pitsə 〕 *n.* 披薩
A *pizza* was delivered to my home.

place 〔 ples 〕 *n.* 地方
This is the *place* where we traveled.

plain 〔 plen 〕 *adj.* 簡單的 *n.* 平原
I wrote an essay in *plain* language.
There are *plains* in central Canada.

plan 〔 plæn 〕 *v. n.* 計劃
Eve *planned* to study abroad.

plane 〔 plen 〕 *n.* 飛機
You have to go abroad by *plane*.

planet (ˈplænɪt) *n.* 行星
Our earth is one of the *planets* in the solar system.

plant (plænt) *n.* 植物 *v.* 種植
The mango is a tropical *plant*.
We are going to *plant* trees around the house.

plate (plet) *n.* 盤子
Jim puts a spoon on the *plate*.

platform (ˈplætˌfɔrm) *n.* 月台
We are waiting for him on the *platform*.

play (ple) *v.* 玩 *n.* 戲劇
They are *playing* in the park.
We plan to go to a *play* after lunch.

player (ˈpleɚ) *n.* 球員
There were five *players* on each team.

playground (ˈpleˌgraʊnd) *n.* 操場；遊樂場
A *playground* is a place for children to play.

pleasant (ˈplɛznt) *adj.* 愉快的
I spent a *pleasant* afternoon at the seaside.

please 〔 pliz 〕 *adv.* 請　*v.* 取悅；使高興
Would you *please* help me clean the room?
Nothing *pleased* him.

pleased 〔 plizd 〕 *adj.* 高興的
I'm *pleased* to hear the news.

pleasure 〔'plɛʒɚ 〕 *n.* 樂趣
I've got a lot of *pleasure* from this trip.

plus 〔 plʌs 〕 *prep.* 加上
Three *plus* five is eight.

pocket 〔'pɑkɪt 〕 *n.* 口袋
There are two *pockets* on my pants.

poem 〔'po·ɪm 〕 *n.* 詩
She wrote these *poems*.

point 〔 pɔɪnt 〕 *n.* 點　*v.* 用手指…
What do these *points* on the map stand for?
He *pointed* to the door.

poison 〔'pɔɪzn̩ 〕 *n.* 毒藥
There is *poison* in the bottle.

police ﹝ pəˈlis ﹞ *n.* 警方

The *police* caught the robbers.

policeman ﹝ pəˈlismən ﹞ *n.* 警察（= *cop*）

The *policeman* arrested the thief.

policy ﹝ ˈpɑləsɪ ﹞ *n.* 政策

Honesty is the best *policy*.

polite ﹝ pəˈlaɪt ﹞ *adj.* 有禮貌的

You have to be *polite* when speaking to the
teacher.

pollute ﹝ pəˈlut ﹞ *v.* 污染

The rivers have been *polluted*.

pollution ﹝ pəˈluʃən ﹞ *n.* 污染

There is a lot of *pollution* in the world.

pond ﹝ pɑnd ﹞ *n.* 池塘

There were two dogs drinking from
the *pond*.

pool ﹝ pul ﹞ *n.* 游泳池

There is a swimming *pool* in the front yard.

poor 〔 pʊr 〕 *adj.* 窮的

He is too *poor* to buy a computer.

popcorn 〔'pɑpˌkɔrn 〕 *n.* 爆米花

I love to eat *popcorn* when watching TV.

pop music *n.* 流行音樂

Most people love listening to *pop music*.

popular 〔'pɑpjələ 〕 *adj.* 受歡迎的

"Snow White" is a very *popular* story.

population 〔ˌpɑpjə'leʃən 〕 *n.* 人口

China has a large *population*.

pork 〔 pɔrk 〕 *n.* 豬肉

I hate eating *pork*.

position 〔 pə'zɪʃən 〕 *n.* 位置

Can you find the *position* of New York on this map?

positive 〔'pɑzətɪv 〕 *adj.* 肯定的

He gave me a *positive* answer.

possible 〔'pɑsəbl̩ 〕 *adj.* 可能的

He had tried every *possible* way to find her.

post ﹝ post ﹞ *v.* 張貼   *v.* 郵寄
(= *mail*【美式用法】)

He *posted* a notice on the wall.

Post this letter, please.

post office *n.* 郵局

You can buy stamps at the *post office*.

postcard ﹝'post,kɑrd ﹞ *n.* 明信片

I sent a *postcard* to my friend.

pot ﹝ pɑt ﹞ *n.* 茶壺

This *pot* is made of glass.

potato ﹝ pə'teto ﹞ *n.* 馬鈴薯

We are eating *potato* chips.

pound ﹝ paʊnd ﹞ *n.* 磅

The tomato weighs four *pounds*.

powder ﹝'paʊdɚ ﹞ *n.* 粉

He doesn't like this brand of milk *powder*.

power ﹝'paʊɚ ﹞ *n.* 力量

Carrying this heavy box requires a lot of *power*.

powerful ('pauə·fəl) *adj.* 強有力的
Jimmy has a *powerful* forearm.

practice ('præktɪs) *v.* 練習
(= *practise*【英式用法】)
Helen *practices* basketball every afternoon.

praise (prez) *v.* 稱讚
My teacher always *praises* me.

pray (pre) *v.* 祈禱
John *prays* before he goes to bed.

precious ('prɛʃəs) *adj.* 珍貴的
Diamonds are *precious* stones.

prefer (prɪ'fɜ) *v.* 比較喜歡
I *prefer* beer above all other drinks.

prepare (prɪ'pɛr) *v.* 準備
Fred *prepares* his own breakfast in the
morning.

present ('prɛznt) *n.* 禮物　*adj.* 出席的
This guitar would be a great Christmas *present*.
A lot of students were *present* at the meeting.

president (ˈprɛzədənt) *n.* 總統
The *president* gave a speech on TV.

press (prɛs) *v.* 按；壓 *n.* 新聞界
Please *press* this button.
The *press* is concerned about this matter.

pressure (ˈprɛʃɚ) *n.* 壓力
He works best under *pressure*.

pretty (ˈprɪtɪ) *adj.* 漂亮的
Emma is a *pretty* girl.

price (praɪs) *n.* 價格
She is looking at the *price* of the dress.

priest (prist) *n.* 牧師
That man is a *priest*, isn't he?

primary (ˈpraɪˌmɛrɪ) *adj.* 初等的；主要的
A *primary* school is a school for children
between the ages of 5 and 11.
I don't know the *primary* purpose of his visit.

prince (prɪns) *n.* 王子
A *prince* is the son of a king and a queen.

princess（'prɪnsɪs）*n.* 公主
A *princess* is the daughter of a king and a queen.

principal（'prɪnsəpḷ）*n.* 校長
Mr. Brown is the *principal* of our school.

principle（'prɪnsəpḷ）*n.* 原則；原理
I don't understand the *principles* of economics.

print（prɪnt）*v.* 印刷
Many books are *printed* for use in schools.

printer（'prɪntɚ）*n.* 印表機
I bought a new *printer* last night.

prison（'prɪzṇ）*n.* 監獄
The robber was sent to *prison*.

prisoner（'prɪzṇɚ）*n.* 囚犯
There were many *prisoners* of war in this camp.

private（'praɪvɪt）*adj.* 私人的
This is my *private* room.

prize ﹝ praɪz ﹞ *n.* 獎；獎品
He won the first *prize*.

probably ﹙'prɑbəblɪ﹚ *adv.* 大概
He will *probably* come.

problem ﹙'prɑbləm﹚ *n.* 問題
They have a *problem* they cannot solve.

produce ﹝ prə'djus ﹞ *v.* 生產
The factory *produces* 15,000 cars a month.

product ﹙'prɑdəkt﹚ *n.* 產品
This company produces many natural
products.

production ﹝ prə'dʌkʃən ﹞ *n.* 產量
Production fell off last year but it is up again
now.

professor ﹝ prə'fɛsə ﹞ *n.* 教授
She is a *professor* of physics at my university.

program ﹙'progræm﹚ *n.* 節目
(= *programme* 【英式用法】)
"Friends" is my favorite TV *program*.

progress 〔 prəˈgrɛs 〕 v. 進步 〔ˈprɑgrɛs 〕 n.
Students need to *progress* in their studying.

project 〔ˈprɑdʒɛkt 〕 n. 計劃
The bridge is a *project* of Japan.

promise 〔ˈprɑmɪs 〕 v. 保證
He *promised* to wait till I came back.

pronounce 〔 prəˈnaʊns 〕 v. 發音
How do you *pronounce* this word?

propose 〔 prəˈpoz 〕 v. 提議
He *proposed* taking a rest here.

protect 〔 prəˈtɛkt 〕 v. 保護
My father always *protects* me.

protection 〔 prəˈtɛkʃən 〕 n. 保護
Children live under the *protection* of their
parents.

proud 〔 praʊd 〕 adj. 驕傲的
They are *proud* that she is doing well at school.

prove 〔 pruv 〕 v. 證明
I can *prove* his innocence.

provide (prə'vaɪd) v. 提供
They didn't *provide* me with any details.

public ('pʌblɪk) adj. 公共的
You mustn't do that in a *public* place.

pull (pʊl) v. 拉
I *pulled* her up from the river.

pump (pʌmp) n. 抽水機
We use a *pump* to draw water.

pumpkin ('pʌmpkɪn) n. 南瓜
Pumpkin pies are tasty.

punish ('pʌnɪʃ) v. 處罰
Sam's parents *punished* him for being bad.

puppy ('pʌpɪ) n. 小狗
A lot of *puppies* were sold at the night market.

purchase ('pɝtʃəs) v. 購買
They *purchased* a lot of things in that grocery story.

purple ('pɝpl̩) adj. 紫色的
She has a *purple* shirt.

purpose ('pɝpəs) *n.* 目的
The *purpose* of going to school is to learn.

purse (pɝs) *n.* 錢包
A *purse* is a very small bag.

push (puʃ) *v.* 推
They *pushed* him into the car.

put (put) *v.* 放
He *put* down a heavy bag.

puzzle ('pʌzl̩) *v.* 使困惑
He was *puzzled* and couldn't answer the question.

Q q

quality ('kwɑlətɪ) *n.* 品質
Quality matters more than quantity.

quarter ('kwɔrtɚ) *n.* 四分之一
He has walked a *quarter* of a mile.

queen (kwin) *n.* 皇后
The *queen* is the king's wife.

question ('kwɛstʃən) *n.* 問題
May I ask you a *question*?

quick (kwɪk) *adj.* 快的
I'm not a *quick* runner.

quiet ('kwaɪət) *adj.* 安靜的
Sally is a *quiet* child.

quit (kwɪt) *v.* 戒除
He has to *quit* smoking.

quite (kwaɪt) *adv.* 非常
He is *quite* sick, so he can't go to school today.

quiz (kwɪz) *n.* 小考
We'll have a *quiz* in math class tomorrow.

R r

rabbit ('ræbɪt) *n.* 兔子
Adam feeds his *rabbits* twice a day.

race (res) *n.* 賽跑；比賽
He came in second in the *race*.

radio (´redɪ‚o) *n.* 收音機

My father listens to the *radio* early in the morning.

railroad (´rel‚rod) *n.* 鐵路

(= *railway*【英式用法】)

A new *railroad* is being built.

railway (´rel‚we) *n.* 鐵路

Don't walk along the *railway*.

rain (ren) *n.* 雨

The ground is wet because of the *rain*.

rainbow (´ren‚bo) *n.* 彩虹

There are seven colors in the *rainbow*.

raincoat (´ren‚kot) *n.* 雨衣

Cathy has to put on a *raincoat* because it is raining.

rainy (´renɪ) *adj.* 下雨的

Today is a *rainy* day.

raise (rez) *v.* 舉起；提高；養育

Jennifer is the first to *raise* her hand.

range (rendʒ) *n.* 範圍

There is a wide price *range* for books.

rapid ('ræpɪd) *adj.* 快速的

He took a *rapid* glance at me.

rare (rɛr) *adj.* 罕見的

These flowers are very *rare* in this country.

rat (ræt) *n.* 老鼠

The *rats* have made holes in those bags
of rice.

rather ('ræðɚ) *adv.* 寧願

I'd *rather* stay than go.

reach (ritʃ) *v.* 到達

We *reached* the airport in time.

read (rid) *v.* 閱讀

Dad *reads* the newspaper every morning.

ready ('rɛdɪ) *adj.* 準備好的

Karen is not *ready* for the exam.

real ('riəl) *adj.* 真的

This apple is not *real*.

realize ('riə,laɪz) *v.* 了解

（= *realise*【英式用法】）

Penny didn't *realize* that it was already
Saturday.

really ('riəlɪ) *adv.* 事實上

He looked poor but he is *really* rich.

reason ('rizn̩) *n.* 理由

We have *reason* to believe that he is right.

receive (rɪ'siv) *v.* 收到

Andrew *received* a bicycle from his uncle
yesterday.

recent ('risn̩t) *adj.* 最近的

That is my experience of *recent* years.

recently ('risn̩tlɪ) *adv.* 最近

He came to see me *recently*.

record ('rɛkəd) *n.* 紀錄

He broke the *record* of the one-hundred meter
dash.

recorder (rɪ'kɔrdə) *n.* 錄音機

The *recorder* is out of order.

recover〔rɪ'kʌvə〕v. 恢復
Mary has *recovered* from her illness.

rectangle〔'rɛktæŋgl〕n. 長方形
This table is a *rectangle*.

recycle〔ri'saɪkl〕v. 回收；再利用
The glass from bottles can be *recycled*.

red〔rɛd〕adj. 紅色的
Blood is *red* in color.

refrigerator〔rɪ'frɪdʒə,retə〕n. 冰箱
(= *fridge* = *icebox*)
Keep that cake in the *refrigerator*, please.

refuse〔rɪ'fjuz〕v. 拒絕
Mr. Baker *refuses* to be a secretary.

regard〔rɪ'gɑrd〕v. 認為
The man was *regarded* as a danger to society.

region〔'ridʒən〕n. 地區
Africa is in a tropical *region*.

regret〔rɪ'grɛt〕v. 後悔
Randy *regretted* making his dog so hungry.

regular (ˈrɛgjələ) *adj.* 規律的
Regular exercise is good for your health.

reject (rɪˈdʒɛkt) *v.* 拒絕
The plan was *rejected*.

relative (ˈrɛlətɪv) *n.* 親戚
We went to visit our *relatives* last week.

remember (rɪˈmɛmbə) *v.* 記得
I can't *remember* where I put the pen.

remind (rɪˈmaɪnd) *v.* 提醒
The story *reminds* me of an experience
I had.

rent (rɛnt) *v.* 租
Martin *rented* a boat to go out fishing.

repair (rɪˈpɛr) *v.* 修理
The radio has to be *repaired*.

repeat (rɪˈpit) *v.* 重複；重複說
The teacher *repeated* his words to the class.

reply〔rɪ'plaɪ〕v. 回答
I asked her why she did it, but she did not
reply.

report〔rɪ'port〕n. 報告
We must hand in the *report* on time.

reporter〔rɪ'portɚ〕n. 記者
John's father is a *reporter*.

Republic of China n. 中華民國（ = R.O.C.）
Taiwan is the home of the *R.O.C.*

require〔rɪ'kwaɪr〕v. 需要
They *require* our help.

respect〔rɪ'spɛkt〕v. 尊敬
We *respect* our parents very much.

responsible〔rɪ'spɑnsəbl̩〕adj. 應負責任的
He is *responsible* for the accident.

rest〔rɛst〕v. 休息 pron. 其餘之人（物）
After running for half an hour, Joe sat down
to *rest*.
You can eat up the *rest* of the meal.

restaurant (ˈrɛstərənt) *n.* 餐廳
A lot of people have their lunch in the *restaurant*.

restroom (ˈrɛstˌrum) *n.* 洗手間
(= *rest room*)
Let's ask the person where the *restroom* is.

result (rɪˈzʌlt) *n.* 結果
What was the *result* of the game?

return (rɪˈtɜn) *v.* 歸還
Please *return* the book I lent you.

review (rɪˈvju) *v.* 複習
Let's *review* today's lesson.

revise (rɪˈvaɪz) *v.* 修正；修訂
The writer *revised* his story.

rice (raɪs) *n.* 米飯
The children like to eat *rice* more than noodles.

rich (rɪtʃ) *adj.* 有錢的
Bill Gates is a *rich* man.

ride ﹝ raɪd ﹞ v. 騎
The small boy is *riding* a bicycle.

right ﹝ raɪt ﹞ *adj.* 正確的；右邊的 *n.* 權利
Show me the *right* way to do it.
You have no *right* to choose.

ring ﹝ rɪŋ ﹞ v. (鈴) 響 *n.* 戒指
Didn't the telephone *ring*?
He bought her a *ring*.

rise ﹝ raɪz ﹞ v. 上升
The sun *rises* in the east.

river ﹝ ˈrɪvɚ ﹞ *n.* 河流
Rivers carry water into the sea or a lake.

road ﹝ rod ﹞ *n.* 道路
Don't play on the *road*.

rob ﹝ rɑb ﹞ v. 搶劫
Farmers were *robbed* of their rice.

robot ﹝ ˈrobət ﹞ *n.* 機器人
A *robot* can do things like a human being.

rock〔rɑk〕*n.* 岩石　*v.* 搖動
They sat down on a flat *rock*.
She *rocked* her baby in her arms.

role〔rol〕*n.* 角色
She played the *role* of Snow White.

roll〔rol〕*v.* 滾動
The ball *rolled* over and over.

roller skates *n. pl.* 輪式溜冰鞋
　(*cf.* rollerblades 直排輪)
He bought a pair of *roller skates* yesterday.

roof〔ruf〕*n.* 屋頂
There is a kitten on the *roof* of the house.

room〔rum〕*n.* 房間；空間
Walter lives in a big house with many *rooms*.

root〔rut〕*n.* 根
Roots hold the plant in the soil.

rope〔rop〕*n.* 繩子
Edward uses a *rope* to tie the boat.

rose ﹝ roz ﹞ *n.* 玫瑰
Roses are beautiful, sweet-smelling flowers.

round ﹝ raʊnd ﹞ *adj.* 圓的
Mary is wearing *round* glasses.

row ﹝ ro ﹞ *n.* 排；列 *v.* 划 (船)
The students stood in two *rows*.
Let's *row* a boat.

royal ﹝ˈrɔɪəl﹞ *adj.* 皇家的
The prince lives in a *royal* palace.

rub ﹝ rʌb ﹞ *v.* 摩擦
The cat *rubbed* its back against my leg.

rubber ﹝ˈrʌbɚ﹞ *n.* 橡膠
Balloons are made of *rubber*.

rude ﹝ rud ﹞ *adj.* 無禮的
It's *rude* to eat and talk at the same time.

ruin ﹝ˈruɪn﹞ *v.* 破壞
The typhoon *ruined* the city.

rule ﹝ rul ﹞ *v.* 統治
The king *ruled* the country for many years.

ruler 〔'rulɚ〕 *n.* 尺；統治者
He drew lines with a *ruler*.

run 〔 rʌn 〕 *v.* 跑
Kate can *run* very fast.

rush 〔 rʌʃ 〕 *v.* 趕忙前往；衝
Linda *rushed* to school.

Russia 〔'rʌʃə〕 *n.* 俄國
They went to *Russia* last year.

Russian 〔'rʌʃən〕 *adj.* 俄國的
She is a *Russian* dancer.

S s

sad 〔 sæd 〕 *adj.* 悲傷的
I always cry whenever I see a *sad* movie.

safe 〔 sef 〕 *adj.* 安全的   *n.* 保險箱
This street is *safe* for walking.
Dad has a fireproof *safe*.

safety 〔'seftɪ〕 *n.* 安全
We put money in a bank for *safety*.

sail 〔 sel 〕 *v.* 航行

The ship *sails* slowly into the harbor.

sailor 〔'selɚ 〕 *n.* 水手

I saw a *sailor* walking near the port.

salad 〔'sæləd 〕 *n.* 沙拉

I like to eat s*alad*.

sale 〔 sel 〕 *n.* 出售

Mr. Dawson's car is for *sale*.

salesman 〔'selzmən 〕 *n.* 售貨員

Two *salesmen* were showing people sweaters.

salt 〔 sɔlt 〕 *n.* 鹽

Pass me the *salt*, please.

same 〔 sem 〕 *adj.* 相同的

We always go to the *same* place after work.

sample 〔'sæmpḷ 〕 *n.* 範例

Teachers give a *sample* of the exam.

sand 〔 sænd 〕 *n.* 沙

She got some *sand* in her eye.

sandwich ﹝'sændwɪtʃ﹞ *n.* 三明治
We can find fish *sandwiches* at McDonald's.

satisfy ﹝'sætɪsˌfaɪ﹞ *v.* 滿足
The government can't fully *satisfy* people's needs.

Saturday ﹝'sætədɪ﹞ *n.* 星期六（= *Sat.*）
Saturday comes after Friday.

saucer ﹝'sɔsə﹞ *n.* 碟子
She offered me tea in her best cup and *saucer*.

save ﹝sev﹞ *v.* 拯救；節省
Jacky *saved* Judy from drowning.

say ﹝se﹞ *v.* 說
No one can *say* this in French.

scale ﹝skel﹞ *n.* 規模；(*pl.*) 磅秤
The business is large in *scale*.
He weighed himself on the bathroom *scale*.

scared ﹝skɛrd﹞ *adj.* 害怕的
Don't be *scared*.

scarf ﹝ skɑrf ﹞ *n.* 圍巾

Adam bought a *scarf* from a clothing shop.

scene ﹝ sin ﹞ *n.* 景色

The boats in the harbor make a beautiful *scene*.

scenery ﹝ 'sinərɪ ﹞ *n.* 風景

We stopped to admire the *scenery*.

school ﹝ skul ﹞ *n.* 學校

We go to *school* five days a week.

science ﹝ 'saɪəns ﹞ *n.* 科學

I'll study *science* in the next class.

scientist ﹝ 'saɪəntɪst ﹞ *n.* 科學家

My uncle is a *scientist*.

scooter ﹝ 'skutɚ ﹞ *n.* 滑板車

My mother bought me a *scooter* for my birthday.

score ﹝ skor ﹞ *n.* 分數

The teacher blamed her for her low *score*.

screen ﹝ skrin ﹞ *n.* 螢幕
There is a spot on the TV *screen*.

sea ﹝ si ﹞ *n.* 海
Is the *sea* here warm enough for swimming?

seafood ﹝'si‚fud ﹞ *n.* 海鮮
Seafood is my father's favorite.

search ﹝ sɜtʃ ﹞ *v.* 尋找
Peter is *searching* for his watch.

season ﹝'sizn̩ ﹞ *n.* 季節
There are four *seasons* in a year.

seat ﹝ sit ﹞ *n.* 座位
Alisa gave her *seat* on the bus to an old
woman.

second ﹝'sɛkənd ﹞ *adj.* 第二的　*n.* 秒
The *second* prize was given to William.
There are sixty *seconds* in a minute.

secondary ﹝'sɛkən‚dɛrɪ ﹞ *adj.* 第二的；次要的
This thing is *secondary* to that.

secret ('sikrɪt) *n.* 祕密
She can't keep a *secret*.

secretary ('sɛkrə,tɛrɪ) *n.* 秘書
She is the private *secretary* of my boss.

section ('sɛkʃən) *n.* 部分
Mother cut the pie into eight equal *sections*.

see (si) *v.* 看見
I can't *see* the blackboard clearly.

seed (sid) *n.* 種子
We sowed vegetable *seeds* in the garden.

seek (sik) *v.* 尋找
He is *seeking* a new job.

seem (sim) *v.* 似乎
This exam *seems* hard to her.

seesaw ('si,sɔ) *n.* 翹翹板
The kids are playing on a *seesaw* at the playground.

seldom ('sɛldəm) *adv.* 很少
I *seldom* go out at night.

select 〔 sə'lɛkt 〕 v. 挑選

John *selected* a present for his girlfriend.

selfish 〔'sɛlfɪʃ 〕 adj. 自私的

After he was bankrupt, he became *selfish*.

sell 〔 sɛl 〕 v. 賣

Judy *sold* her land to pay debts.

semester 〔 sə'mɛstɚ 〕 n. 學期

I want to take French class next *semester*.

send 〔 sɛnd 〕 v. 寄；送

I *sent* a greeting card to my sister.

senior high school n. 高中

My brother studies in a famous *senior high school*.

sense 〔 sɛns 〕 n. 感覺；感官

Our five *senses* are sight, hearing, taste, smell, and touch.

separate 〔'sɛpərɪt 〕 adj. 分開的

Our teeth are *separate*.

sentence ('sɛntəns) *n.* 句子
Please make a *sentence* with the word.

September (sɛp'tɛmbɚ) *n.* 九月 (= *Sep.*)
Lisa's birthday is in *September*.

serious ('sɪrɪəs) *adj.* 嚴重的
Tom had a *serious* car accident yesterday.

servant ('sɝvənt) *n.* 僕人
Policemen are public *servants*.

serve (sɝv) *v.* 服務
The cook *served* the Brown family for
one year.

service ('sɝvɪs) *n.* 服務
The *service* in this restaurant is very good.

set (sɛt) *v.* 設定　*n.* 一組；一套
We must *set* the time for the meeting.
I want to buy a *set* of dishes.

seven ('sɛvən) *adj.* 七個
There are *seven* days in a week.

seventeen〔͵sɛvən'tin〕*adj.* 十七的
Sam's elder brother is *seventeen* years old.

seventeenth〔͵sɛvən'tinθ〕*adj.* 第十七的
I'm the *seventeenth* to get a ticket.

seventh〔'sɛvənθ〕*adj.* 第七的
This is Beethoven's *seventh* symphony.

seventy〔'sɛvəntɪ〕*adj.* 七十個
There are *seventy* people in my class.

several〔'sɛvərəl〕*adj.* 好幾個
Several boys took part in the race.

shake〔ʃek〕*v.* 搖
You should *shake* the can before drinking.

shall〔ʃæl〕*aux.* 將
After 10:00 p.m., Nancy *shall* call you again.

shape〔ʃep〕*n.* 形狀
The shell has a strange *shape*.

share 〔 ∫εr 〕 v. 分享
My friend *shares* a cake with me.

shark 〔 ∫ɑrk 〕 n. 鯊魚
No one can catch the *shark*.

sharp 〔 ∫ɑrp 〕 adj. 銳利的
The knife is very *sharp*.

she 〔 ∫i 〕 pron. 她
She is a nurse.

sheep 〔 ∫ip 〕 n. 羊
John keeps a lot of *sheep*.

sheet 〔 ∫it 〕 n. 紙張
You should write it on a *sheet* of paper.

shelf 〔 ∫εlf 〕 n. 架子
I took some books off the *shelf*.

shine 〔 ∫aɪn 〕 v. 照耀
The sun was *shining* brightly.

ship 〔 ∫ɪp 〕 n. 船 v. 運送
Ships carry passengers over the sea.
The books were *shipped* by truck.

shirt 〔 ʃɜt 〕 *n.* 襯衫

This shop sells sports *shirts*.

shock 〔 ʃɑk 〕 *n.* 震驚   *v.* 使震驚

Her death was a great *shock* to me.

His behavior *shocked* me.

shoe 〔 ʃu 〕 *n.* 鞋子

I wore a new pair of *shoes* this morning.

shoot 〔 ʃut 〕 *v.* 射擊

He was *shot* in the arm.

shop 〔 ʃɑp 〕 *n.* 商店 (= *store*)   *v.* 購物

This flower *shop* opens at 6:00 a.m.

I will go *shopping* in the afternoon.

shopkeeper 〔 'ʃɑpˌkipɚ 〕 *n.* 商店老闆

The *shopkeeper* could manage this shop very well.

shore 〔 ʃor 〕 *n.* 海岸

The waves washed over the *shore*.

short 〔 ʃɔrt 〕 *adj.* 短的

He finished his homework in a very *short* time.

shorts〔ʃɔrts〕*n.pl.* 短褲
She wore *shorts* to play volleyball.

shot〔ʃɑt〕*n.* 射擊
He fired five *shots*.

should〔ʃʊd〕*aux.* 應該
You *should* take a rest.

shoulder〔'ʃoldɚ〕*n.* 肩膀
His *shoulder* was hurt in an accident.

shout〔ʃaʊt〕*v.* 大叫
My friend *shouted* at me yesterday.

show〔ʃo〕*v.* 給（某人）看
He *showed* me his album.

shower〔'ʃaʊɚ〕*n.* 淋浴
I take a *shower* every morning.

shrimp〔ʃrɪmp〕*n.* 蝦子
There are a lot of *shrimp* in the river.

shut〔ʃʌt〕*v.* 關閉
Strong wind *shut* the door.

shy 〔 ʃaɪ 〕 *adj.* 害羞的

I'm too *shy* to speak to strangers.

sick 〔 sɪk 〕 *adj.* 生病的

He is *sick* with a cold.

side 〔 saɪd 〕 *n.* 邊

You must walk on one *side* of the road.

sidewalk 〔'saɪd,wɔk 〕 *n.* 人行道

　(= *pavement* 〔'pevmənt 〕【英式用法】)

She fell on the icy *sidewalk*.

sight 〔 saɪt 〕 *n.* 景象

The lake was a beautiful *sight*.

sign 〔 saɪn 〕 *v.* 簽名　　*n.* 告示牌

Helen *signed* her name.

The *sign* says, "No Smoking."

silence 〔'saɪləns 〕 *n.* 沉默

Speech is silver, *silence* is golden.

silent 〔'saɪlənt 〕 *adj.* 沉默的；不出聲的

The teacher told the students to be *silent*.

silly (ˈsɪlɪ) *adj.* 愚蠢的
Mother lets me play a *silly* game.

silver (ˈsɪlvɚ) *n.* 銀
That ring is made of *silver*.

similar (ˈsɪmələ) *adj.* 類似的
Her dress is *similar* to yours in style.

simple (ˈsɪmpl̩) *adj.* 簡單的
This book is written in *simple* English.

simply (ˈsɪmplɪ) *adv.* 只是
He worked *simply* to get money.

since (sɪns) *prep.* 自從
It has been raining *since* five in the morning.

sincere (sɪnˈsɪr) *adj.* 眞誠的
I accepted a *sincere* apology.

sing (sɪŋ) *v.* 唱歌
We often *sing* a song in music class.

Singapore (ˈsɪŋgəˌpor) *n.* 新加坡
My uncle lives in *Singapore*.

singer ('sɪŋɚ) *n.* 歌手
Madonna is my favorite *singer*.

single ('sɪŋgḷ) *adj.* 單身的
John is still *single*.

sink (sɪŋk) *n.* 洗手台 *v.* 下沉
Sinks are used for washing dishes.
The ship *sank*.

sir (sɝ) *n.* 先生
Good luck to you, *sir*.

sister ('sɪstɚ) *n.* 姊妹
My little *sister* is a clever girl.

sit (sɪt) *v.* 坐
Please *sit* down.

six (sɪks) *n.* 六
Five plus one equals *six*.

sixteen (sɪks'tin) *adj.* 十六的
Kate's brother is *sixteen* years old.

sixteenth 〔 sɪks'tinθ 〕 *adj.* 第十六的
Harry's birthday is the *sixteenth* of December.

sixth 〔 sɪksθ 〕 *adj.* 第六的
June is the *sixth* month of the year.

sixty 〔 'sɪkstɪ 〕 *adj.* 六十的
My grandmother is *sixty* years old.

size 〔 saɪz 〕 *n.* 尺寸；大小
What *size* do you wear?

skate 〔 sket 〕 *v.* 溜冰
Most young people enjoy *skating*.

ski 〔 ski 〕 *v.* 滑雪
He likes *skiing* very much.

skill 〔 skɪl 〕 *n.* 技巧
Zoe showed us her *skill* at cooking.

skillful 〔 'skɪlfəl 〕 *adj.* 熟練的
She is *skillful* at drawing.

skin 〔 skɪn 〕 *n.* 皮膚
She has beautiful *skin*.

skinny ('skɪnɪ) *adj.* 皮包骨的
Tony is a *skinny* boy.

skirt (skɜt) *n.* 裙子
Patrick bought his girlfriend a *skirt*.

sky (skaɪ) *n.* 天空
Birds fly across the *sky*.

sleep (slip) *v.* 睡覺
Anna *sleeps* well after a long trip.

sleepy ('slipɪ) *adj.* 想睡的
I feel very *sleepy*.

slender ('slɛndɚ) *adj.* 苗條的
My mother is a *slender* woman.

slide (slaɪd) *v.* 滑動
A car *slides* along the road.

slim (slɪm) *adj.* 苗條的
She is very *slim* because she swims every week.

slip (slɪp) *v.* 滑   *n.* 紙片;紙條
The book *slipped* off my knees.
Write your name on this pink *slip*.

slippers ('slɪpəz) *n. pl.* 拖鞋
Joy wears *slippers* for a comfortable walk.

slow (slo) *adj.* 慢的
My watch is two minutes *slow*.

small (smɔl) *adj.* 小的
There is a *small* house behind the mountain.

smart (smɑrt) *adj.* 聰明的
Victor is explaining his *smart* idea.

smell (smɛl) *v.* 聞
Jenny *smelled* the rose with her nose.

smile (smaɪl) *v.* 微笑
Remember to *smile* when I take your picture.

smoke (smok) *n.* 煙
The kitchen was filled with black *smoke*.

snack (snæk) *n.* 點心;零食
Sam wants to eat a *snack* before dinner.

snail (snel) *n.* 蝸牛
There are *snails* in the garden.

snake 〔 snek 〕 *n.* 蛇
Snakes have long and thin bodies.

sneakers 〔'snikəz 〕 *n. pl.* 膠底運動鞋
Wearing *sneakers* is very comfortable.

sneaky 〔'snikɪ 〕 *adj.* 鬼鬼祟祟的；卑鄙的
Jill is *sneaky*, so don't trust her.

snow 〔 sno 〕 *n.* 雪
The *snow* came late this year.

snowman 〔'snomæn 〕 *n.* 雪人
We made a *snowman* in the front yard.

snowy 〔'snoɪ 〕 *adj.* 多雪的
We are going to have a *snowy* winter this year.

so 〔 so 〕 *adv.* 非常地　*conj.* 所以
I'm *so* tired after running.
It was raining, *so* I took an umbrella with me.

soap 〔 sop 〕 *n.* 肥皂
She washed her hands with *soap*.

soccer 〔'sɑkə 〕 *n.* 足球
A lot of boys love playing *soccer*.

social ('soʃəl) *adj.* 社會的；社交的
Unemployment is a *social* problem.

society (sə'saɪətɪ) *n.* 社會
Chinese *society* is now changing.

socks (saks) *n. pl.* 短襪
We put on our *socks* before our shoes.

soda ('sodə) *n.* 汽水
I would like a glass of *soda*.

sofa ('sofə) *n.* 沙發
Mary is sitting on the *sofa* and reading a book.

soft (sɔft) *adj.* 柔軟的
Which would you like better? A *soft* mattress
or a hard one?

soft drink *n.* 不含酒精的飲料
Would you like a *soft drink*?

softball ('sɔft,bɔl) *n.* 壘球
We are playing *softball* now.

soldier ('soldʒɚ) *n.* 軍人
Peter is a *soldier*.

solution 〔 sə'luʃən 〕 *n.* 解決之道
We have to find a *solution* as soon as possible.

solve 〔 sɑlv 〕 *v.* 解決
Michael is trying to *solve* the problem.

some 〔 sʌm 〕 *adj.* 一些
My sister wants to drink *some* milk.

somebody 〔'sʌm,bɑdɪ 〕 *pron.* 有人；某人
(= *someone*)
Somebody wants to see you.

someone 〔'sʌm,wʌn 〕 *pron.* 某人
(= *somebody*)
I saw *someone* walking in front of your house.

something 〔'sʌmθɪŋ 〕 *pron.* 某事
I had *something* to tell you, but I forgot.

sometimes 〔'sʌm,taɪmz 〕 *adv.* 有時候
Sometimes it rains in the morning.

somewhere 〔'sʌm,hwɛr 〕 *adv.* 某處
Fred has left his books *somewhere* in the school.

son ﹝ sʌn ﹞ *n.* 兒子
She has two *sons* and one daughter.

song ﹝ sɔŋ ﹞ *n.* 歌曲
Karen really loves to write *songs*.

soon ﹝ sun ﹞ *adv.* 很快地
I hope we will get there *soon*.

sore ﹝ sor ﹞ *adj.* 疼痛的
I have a *sore* throat.

sorry ﹝'sɔrɪ ﹞ *adj.* 抱歉的
I'm *sorry* to hurt you.

sort ﹝ sɔrt ﹞ *n.* 種類　*v.* 將⋯分類
I like this *sort* of house.
Sort these cards according to their colors.

soul ﹝ sol ﹞ *n.* 靈魂
Many people believe that a man's *soul* never
dies.

sound ﹝ saʊnd ﹞ *n.* 聲音
I heard a strange *sound*.

soup〔 sup 〕 *n.* 湯
Henry asked for a bowl of *soup*.

sour 〔 saʊr 〕 *adj.* 酸的
This lemon is very *sour*.

source 〔 sɔrs 〕 *n.* 來源
I don't know the *source* of the information.

south 〔 saʊθ 〕 *n.* 南方
Mexico is to the *south* of the United States.

southern 〔'sʌðən 〕 *adj.* 南方的
We went to *southern* Taiwan last month.

soy sauce *n.* 醬油
I love to eat food with *soy sauce*.

space 〔 spes 〕 *n.* 空間
Our new house has more *space*.

spaghetti 〔 spə'gɛtɪ 〕 *n.* 義大利麵
I think I'll have *spaghetti* with meatballs.

speak 〔 spik 〕 *v.* 說
Michelle can *speak* Spanish.

speaker (ˈspikɚ) *n.* 演講者

He is a good *speaker*.

special (ˈspɛʃəl) *adj.* 特別的

He surprised his wife with a *special* gift.

speech (spitʃ) *n.* 演講

Ted gave a *speech* in front of his classmates.

speed (spid) *n.* 速度

The *speed* of this train is 200 kilometers an hour.

spell (spɛl) *v.* 拼（字）

He *spells* his name for me.

spelling (ˈspɛlɪŋ) *n.* 拼字；拼寫能力

Her *spelling* has improved.

spend (spɛnd) *v.* 花費

Nick *spends* so much money on traveling.

spider (ˈspaɪdɚ) *n.* 蜘蛛

Judy is afraid of *spiders*.

spirit (ˈspɪrɪt) *n.* 精神

She lost her *spirit* after his death.

spoon〔 spun 〕*n.* 湯匙
People use *spoons* for eating.

sport〔 sport 〕*n.* 運動
Soccer is the favorite *sport* of English people.

sports〔 sports 〕*adj.* 運動的
I bought a pair of *sports* shoes yesterday.

spot〔 spɑt 〕*n.* 地點 *v.* 發現
Don't go to the dangerous *spot*.
I *spotted* my friend at once in the crowd.

spread〔 sprɛd 〕*v. n.* 散播；蔓延
The news *spread* quickly.
We should stop the *spread* of the disease.

spring〔 sprɪŋ 〕*n.* 春天
Mandy will come back home in *spring*.

square〔 skwɛr 〕*n.* 正方形
The paper was cut into *squares*.

stage〔 stedʒ 〕*n.* 舞台
He doesn't like to stand on the *stage*.

stairs ﹝stɛrz﹞ *n.pl.* 樓梯
Tom is going down the *stairs*.

stamp ﹝stæmp﹞ *n.* 郵票
Stamp collecting is my hobby.

stand ﹝stænd﹞ *v.* 站著
Don't *stand* there; I can't see the television.

standard ﹝'stændəd﹞ *n.* 標準 *adj.* 標準的
His work was below the required *standard*.
We should learn *standard* English.

star ﹝stɑr﹞ *n.* 星星
There are many *stars* in the sky tonight.

start ﹝stɑrt﹞ *v.* 開始
The bank machine will *start* working next
Monday.

state ﹝stet﹞ *n.* 州
There are fifty *states* in the U.S.A.

station ﹝'steʃən﹞ *n.* 車站
I parked my car at the *station*.

stationery ('steʃənˌɛrɪ) *n.* 文具
I want to have my own *stationery* store.

stay (ste) *v.* 暫住
My sister *stays* at my apartment.

steak (stek) *n.* 牛排
The waiter is serving me *steak*.

steal (stil) *v.* 偷
Jimmy has *stolen* my car.

steam (stim) *n.* 蒸氣
Boiled water becomes *steam*.

step (stɛp) *n.* 步驟
We should take *steps* to stop it.

stick (stɪk) *n.* 棍子
He held a *stick* in his hand.

still (stɪl) *adv.* 仍然
They *still* do not know the result.

stingy ('stɪndʒɪ) *adj.* 小氣的
Don't be so *stingy* with the butter.

stomach ('stʌmək) *n.* 胃 (= *tummy* ('tʌmɪ))
The food we eat goes into our *stomach*.

stomachache ('stʌmək,ek) *n.* 胃痛
A *stomachache* is very painful.

stone (ston) *n.* 石頭
He picked up a *stone* and threw it at the dog.

stop (stɑp) *v.* 停止
The car *stops* at the red light.

store (stor) *n.* 商店 *v.* 儲存
Mother took us to the shoe *store* to buy shoes.
We *stored* some food for an emergency.

storm (stɔrm) *n.* 暴風雨
The *storm* caused great damage.

stormy ('stɔrmɪ) *adj.* 暴風雨的
It was a *stormy* night.

story ('storɪ) *n.* 故事
Harry Potter is the *story* of a little wizard.

stove (stov) *n.* 火爐
An old man was making a fire in the *stove*.

straight 〔 stret 〕 *adj.* 直的

She has beautiful long *straight* hair.

strange 〔 strendʒ 〕 *adj.* 奇怪的

It's a *strange* story about a cat and a mouse.

stranger 〔'strendʒɚ 〕 *n.* 陌生人

His dog barks at *strangers*.

straw 〔 strɔ 〕 *n.* 稻草

The roof is made of *straw*.

strawberry 〔'strɔ,bɛrɪ 〕 *n.* 草莓

I love to eat toast with *strawberry* jam.

stream 〔 strim 〕 *n.* 小溪

A small *stream* runs in front of our garden.

street 〔 strit 〕 *n.* 街道

There is a library on the *street* where I live.

stress 〔 strɛs 〕 *n.* 壓力　　 *v.* 強調

The examination put a lot of *stress* on him.
He *stressed* the importance of health.

strike 〔 straɪk 〕 *v.* 打

The small boy tried to *strike* me with a stick.

strong ﹝ strɔŋ ﹞ *adj.* 強壯的
He has *strong* arms.

struggle ﹝ ˈstrʌgl̩ ﹞ *v.* 掙扎   *n.* 掙扎；努力
The cat *struggled* in his arms.
Don't give up without a *struggle*.

student ﹝ ˈstjudn̩t ﹞ *n.* 學生
The teacher punished the lazy *student*.

study ﹝ ˈstʌdɪ ﹞ *v.* 研讀
Andrew *studies* English by himself.

stupid ﹝ ˈstjupɪd ﹞ *adj.* 愚蠢的
Laura gave me a *stupid* idea.

style ﹝ staɪl ﹞ *n.* 方式
You'd better change your *style* of living.

subject ﹝ ˈsʌbdʒɪkt ﹞ *n.* 科目
English is my favorite *subject*.

submarine ﹝ ˈsʌbməˏrin ﹞ *n.* 潛水艇
A *submarine* is a special ship.

subway ('sʌb,we) *n.* 地下鐵
  (= *underground* = *tube* (tjub)【英式英語】
  = *MRT* = *metro* ('mɛtro))
I take the *subway* to school every day.

succeed (sək'sid) *v.* 成功
Our plan has *succeeded*.

success (sək'sɛs) *n.* 成功
His life is full of *success*.

successful (sək'sɛsfəl) *adj.* 成功的
She has a very *successful* career.

such (sʌtʃ) *adj.* 如此的
I've never done *such* a thing before.

sudden ('sʌdn̩) *adj.* 突然的
Judy made a *sudden* decision about going abroad.

suddenly ('sʌdn̩lɪ) *adv.* 突然地
She stood up *suddenly* and went out of the room.

sugar ('ʃugɚ) *n.* 糖
Kate puts *sugar* in her tea.

suggest 〔səg'dʒɛst〕 v. 建議
He *suggested* that we should go home.

suit 〔sut〕 v. 適合　n. 西裝
The dress *suits* you.
He bought a *suit* yesterday.

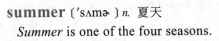

summer 〔'sʌmɚ〕 n. 夏天
Summer is one of the four seasons.

sun 〔sʌn〕 n. 太陽
On a clear day, the *sun* shines brightly in the sky.

Sunday 〔'sʌndɪ〕 n. 星期天 (= *Sun.*)
Sunday comes after Saturday.

sunny 〔'sʌnɪ〕 adj. 晴朗的
Yesterday was very bright and *sunny*.

super 〔'supɚ〕 adj. 極好的；超級的
We had a *super* time.

supermarket 〔'supɚˌmɑrkɪt〕 n. 超級市場
Cheeses are sold in the *supermarket*.

supper 〔'sʌpɚ〕 n. 晚餐 (= *dinner*)
We have *supper* in the evening.

supply ﹝ səˈplaɪ ﹞ *v. n.* 供應

The government *supplied* free books to schools. The *supply* of electricity has been threatened by recent strikes.

support ﹝ səˈport ﹞ *v.* 支持

All of us *supported* him.

sure ﹝ ʃur ﹞ *adj.* 確定的

I'm not *sure* about my answer.

surf ﹝ sɝf ﹞ *v.* 衝浪

My boyfriend is good at *surfing*.

surface ﹝ ˈsɝfɪs ﹞ *n.* 表面

The desk has a smooth *surface*.

surprise ﹝ səˈpraɪz ﹞ *v.* 使驚訝

We will *surprise* Ann with a party on her birthday.

surprised ﹝ səˈpraɪzd ﹞ *adj.* 驚訝的

Jim was *surprised* by her gift.

survive ﹝ səˈvaɪv ﹞ *v.* 存活

When the car crashed, only I *survived*.

swallow (ˈswɑlo) *n.* 燕子 *v.* 吞下
One *swallow* doesn't make a summer.

swan (swɑn) *n.* 天鵝
There are many *swans* living in the lake.

sweater (ˈswɛtɚ) *n.* 毛衣
Sweaters are usually made of wool.

sweep (swip) *v.* 掃
My mother *sweeps* the floor every morning.

sweet (swit) *adj.* 甜美的 *n.* 糖果
(= *candy*)
Ann has a *sweet* voice.
Please help yourself to some *sweets*.

swim (swɪm) *v.* 游泳
You can *swim* wherever you like.

swimsuit (ˈswɪmˌsut) *n.* 泳衣
Mother just bought a new *swimsuit* for my
younger sister.

swing (swɪŋ) *n.* 鞦韆
There are some *swings* in the park.

symbol (ˈsɪmbl̩) *n.* 象徵
Mary designed the *symbol* of our school.

system (ˈsɪstəm) *n.* 系統
We should develop a *system* of our own.

T t

table (ˈtebl̩) *n.* 桌子
Please set the *table* before dinnertime.

table tennis *n.* 桌球
Let's play *table tennis*.

Taichung (ˈtaɪˈtʃuŋ) *n.* 台中
We went to *Taichung* to visit my aunt.

tail (tel) *n.* 尾巴
A monkey has a long *tail*.

Tainan (ˈtaɪˈnɑn) *n.* 台南
I have some relatives who live in *Tainan*.

Taiwan (ˈtaɪˈwɑn) *n.* 台灣
Taiwan is a beautiful island.

Taiwanese (‚taɪwɑˈniz) *n.* 台灣人；台灣話
adj. 台灣人的；台灣話的
Taiwanese is not easy to learn.
Tom wanted to know more about *Taiwanese*
traditions.

take (tek) *v.* 拿
Mike forgot to *take* his book to school.

talent (ˈtælənt) *n.* 才能
She has a *talent* for cooking.

talk (tɔk) *v.* 談話
Andrew and Alan are *talking* on the phone.

talkative (ˈtɔkətɪv) *adj.* 愛說話的
David is such a *talkative* person.

tall (tɔl) *adj.* 高的
George is a *tall* boy.

tangerine (‚tændʒəˈrin) *n.* 橘子
Tangerines are different from oranges.

tank (tæŋk) *n.* 水槽；坦克車
We use *tanks* to store water.

tape 〔 tep 〕 *n.* 錄音帶

He recorded the speech on a *tape*.

target 〔'tɑrgɪt 〕 *n.* 目標   *v.* 將…定作目標

My *target* is to save $200 a month.

The missiles were *targeted* at the enemy capital.

task 〔 tæsk 〕 *n.* 工作；任務

The *task* is not easy.

taste 〔 test 〕 *v.* 嚐起來

This food *tastes* great.

taxi 〔'tæksɪ 〕 *n.* 計程車 (= *taxicab* = *cab*)

You can take a *taxi* to the airport.

tea 〔 ti 〕 *n.* 茶

Mother makes a pot of *tea* for us.

teach 〔 titʃ 〕 *v.* 教

Mr. White *teaches* English.

teacher 〔'titʃɚ 〕 *n.* 老師

Jane's mother is a music *teacher*.

Teacher's Day *n.* 教師節

I sent a card to my teacher on *Teacher's Day*.

team (tim) *n.* 隊

There are eleven people on a football *team*.

teapot ('ti,pɑt) *n.* 茶壺

The *teapots* in the store are so cute.

tear (tɪr) *n.* 眼淚   (tɛr) *v.* 撕裂

Her eyes were filled with *tears*.

He *tore* the envelope open.

teenager ('tin,edʒɚ) *n.* 青少年

Teenagers are boys and girls.

telephone ('tɛlə,fon) *n.* 電話 (= *phone*)

John uses the *telephone* to talk to his friend.

television ('tɛlə,vɪʒən) *n.* 電視 (= *TV*)

Jack watches *television* every night.

tell (tɛl) *v.* 告訴

Please *tell* me the truth.

temperature ('tɛmprətʃɚ) *n.* 溫度

The *temperature* is high in summer.

temple ('tɛmpḷ) *n.* 寺廟
Many people go to the *temple* to pray.

ten (tɛn) *adj.* 十個
There are *ten* fingers on our hands.

tennis ('tɛnɪs) *n.* 網球
Mark is learning to play *tennis*.

tent (tɛnt) *n.* 帳棚
They had lived in *tents* for a few days.

tenth (tɛnθ) *adj.* 第十的
The *tenth* month of the year is October.

term (tɜm) *n.* 期間
Students have to study in the summer *term*.

terrible ('tɛrəbḷ) *adj.* 可怕的
Last night, the storm was *terrible*.

terrific (tə'rɪfɪk) *adj.* 很棒的
It was a *terrific* party.

test (tɛst) *n.* 測驗
We took our English *test* this morning.

textbook ('tɛkst,bʊk) *n.* 教科書
I am studying an English *textbook*.

than (ðæn) *conj.* 比
Sam is taller *than* Paul.

thank (θæŋk) *v.* 感謝
The teacher *thanked* us for giving her some
flowers.

Thanksgiving (,θæŋks'gɪvɪŋ) *n.* 感恩節
(= *Thanksgiving Day*)
Americans eat turkey on *Thanksgiving*.

that (ðæt) *adj.* 那個
I would like to take *that* book.

the (ðə) *art.* 那個
I'm going to *the* post office.

theater ('θiətə) *n.* 戲院 (= *theatre*【英式用法】)
We went to the *theater* last night to watch a
play.

their (ðɛr) *adj.* 他們的
The children like *their* teacher.

theirs 〔 ðɛrz 〕 *pron.* they 的所有代名詞
These pictures are *theirs*.

them 〔 ðɛm 〕 *pron.* they 的受格
The customers gave *them* a tip.

themselves 〔 ðəm'sɛlvz 〕 *pron.*
they 的反身代名詞
Kids can't take care of *themselves*.

then 〔 ðɛn 〕 *adv.* 然後
Close your books and *then* put them away.

there 〔 ðɛr 〕 *adv.* 那裡
There are two apples on the table.

therefore 〔'ðɛr,for 〕 *adv.* 因此
This car is smaller and *therefore* cheaper.

these 〔 ðiz 〕 *adj.* 這些
These books were kept in my room.

they 〔 ðe 〕 *pron.* 他們
They're ready to go to the party.

thick 〔 θɪk 〕 *adj.* 厚的
I have never read such a *thick* book.

thief〔θif〕*n.* 小偷

A *thief* broke into the house last night.

thin〔θɪn〕*adj.* 瘦的

The poor children are *thin*.

thing〔θɪŋ〕*n.* 事情

There are many *things* to remember.

think〔θɪŋk〕*v.* 想

I *think* she will come here today.

third〔θɝd〕*adj.* 第三的

It's the *third* time that he has come to Japan.

thirsty〔'θɝstɪ〕*adj.* 口渴的

The baby is *thirsty*.

thirteen〔θɝ'tin〕*adj.* 十三的

My cousin is *thirteen*.

thirteenth〔θɝ'tinθ〕*adj.* 第十三

Yesterday was the *thirteenth* of September.

thirtieth〔'θɝtɪɪθ〕*adj.* 第三十

Today is the *thirtieth* of May.

thirty〔'θɝtɪ〕*adj.* 三十的

My aunt is *thirty* years old.

this 〔 ðɪs 〕 *adj.* 這個
This book is not mine.

those 〔 ðoz 〕 *adj.* 那些
Those cars are old.

though 〔 ðo 〕 *conj.* 雖然
I love him *though* he doesn't love me.

thought 〔 θɔt 〕 *n.* 想法
What's your *thought*?

thousand 〔 'θaʊznd 〕 *n.* 千
This watch costs one *thousand* dollars.

three 〔 θri 〕 *adj.* 三個
Sandra and Frank have *three* kids.

throat 〔 θrot 〕 *n.* 喉嚨
When we eat, food passes down our *throat*.

through 〔 θru 〕 *prep.* 通過
The train went *through* some tunnels.

throughout 〔 θru'aʊt 〕 *prep.* 遍及
They searched *throughout* the town for the lost child.

throw (θro) *v.* 丟

Richard *throws* small pieces of stone in
a river.

thumb (θʌm) *n.* 大拇指

I hurt my *thumb* yesterday.

thunder ('θʌndɚ) *n.* 雷

There was *thunder* and lightning last night.

Thursday ('θɝzdɪ) *n.* 星期四

  (= *Thurs.* = *Thur.*)

My daughter was born on *Thursday*.

thus (ðʌs) *adv.* 因此

Thus they judged that he was guilty.

ticket ('tɪkɪt) *n.* 票

Tom made a reservation for movie *tickets*.

tidy ('taɪdɪ) *adj.* 整潔的

Mike's room is very *tidy*.

tie (taɪ) *v.* 綁   *n.* 領帶

I *tied* a bow for my younger sister.

He wore a blue *tie*.

tiger ('taɪgə) *n.* 老虎

A *tiger* is a large animal that lives in the jungle.

till (tɪl) *conj.* 直到 (= *until*)

Don't leave *till* I come back.

time (taɪm) *n.* 時間

It's *time* for dinner.

tiny ('taɪnɪ) *adj.* 微小的

You can see *tiny* stars in the sky.

tip (tɪp) *n.* 祕訣;小費

She gave me a *tip* on how to grow roses.

tired (taɪrd) *adj.* 疲倦的

I'm *tired* from work.

title ('taɪtl̩) *n.* 標題

The *title* of the painting is "The Last Supper."

to (tu) *prep.* 到…

Jim goes *to* school in the morning.

toast (tost) *n.* 吐司

Jam goes well with *toast*.

today ﹝ tə'de ﹞ *n.* 今天
Today is Nancy's birthday.

toe ﹝ to ﹞ *n.* 腳趾
I dropped a book on my big *toe*.

tofu ﹝'tofu ﹞ *n.* 豆腐 (= *bean curd*)
I don't like the smell of stinky *tofu*.

together ﹝ tə'gɛðə ﹞ *adv.* 一起
We can go to the store *together*.

toilet ﹝'tɔɪlɪt ﹞ *n.* 廁所
Toilet has the same meaning as restroom.

tomato ﹝ tə'meto ﹞ *n.* 蕃茄
Tomatoes are used for making ketchup.

tomorrow ﹝ tə'mɑro ﹞ *n.* 明天
Tomorrow is the day that comes after today.

tongue ﹝ tʌŋ ﹞ *n.* 舌頭
The *tongue* is inside our mouth.

tonight ﹝ tə'naɪt ﹞ *adv.* 今晚
Let's go to see a movie *tonight*.

too 〔 tu 〕 *adv.* 太

The elephant is *too* big to be kept as a pet.

tool 〔 tul 〕 *n.* 工具

Mechanics use a variety of *tools*.

tooth 〔 tuθ 〕 *n.* 牙齒（複數形是 teeth〔 tiθ 〕）

We must brush our *teeth* every morning and night.

toothache 〔'tuθ,ek 〕 *n.* 牙痛

I have a *toothache*.

toothbrush 〔'tuθ,brʌʃ 〕 *n.* 牙刷

We clean our teeth with a *toothbrush*.

top 〔 tɑp 〕 *n.* 頂端

He climbed to the *top* of the tree.

topic 〔'tɑpɪk 〕 *n.* 主題

What's the *topic* of this article?

total 〔'totl̩ 〕 *adj.* 全部的；總數的

What is the *total* cost of the trip?

touch 〔 tʌtʃ 〕 *v.* 觸摸

Please don't *touch* any paintings.

tour ﹝ tʊr ﹞ *n.* 旅行

We will go on a *tour* this summer vacation.

toward ﹝ tə'wɔrd ﹞ *prep.* 朝… (= *towards*)

He walked *toward* the door.

towel ﹝'taʊəl ﹞ *n.* 毛巾

Nick carries a *towel* to the beach.

tower ﹝'taʊɚ ﹞ *n.* 塔

There is a *tower* near the port.

town ﹝ taʊn ﹞ *n.* 城鎮

He lives in a small *town*.

toy ﹝ tɔɪ ﹞ *n.* 玩具

Children like to play with *toys*.

trace ﹝ tres ﹞ *n.* 足跡

The snail has left its *trace*.

track ﹝ træk ﹞ *n.* 鐵軌 *v.* 追蹤;追捕到

The train left the *tracks*.
The police *tracked* down the thief.

trade ﹝ tred ﹞ *n.* 貿易

There is a lot of *trade* between countries.

tradition (trə'dɪʃən) *n.* 傳統

It's a Christmas *tradition* to give presents.

traditional (trə'dɪʃənḷ) *adj.* 傳統的

Chinese have a lot of *traditional* customs.

traffic ('træfɪk) *n.* 交通

The *traffic* is very heavy today.

train (tren) *n.* 火車 *v.* 訓練

The *train* arrived on time.

They *trained* the horse for the next race.

train station   *n.* 火車站

I will meet you at the *train station*.

trap (træp) *n.* 陷阱

Some people use a *trap* to catch mice.

trash (træʃ) *n.* 垃圾

There are few *trash* cans on the street.

travel ('trævḷ) *v.* 旅行

I love to go *traveling*.

treasure ('trɛʒɚ) *n.* 寶藏

They were looking for the *treasure* of the ship.

treat ﹝ trit ﹞ *v.* 對待

I don't like the way he *treats* me.

treatment ﹝'tritmənt ﹞ *n.* 對待；治療

I cannot stand such *treatment* any longer.

She is now under medical *treatment*.

tree ﹝ tri ﹞ *n.* 樹

There is an apple *tree* in my garden.

trial ﹝'traɪəl ﹞ *n.* 試驗；審判

We must give the machine a *trial*.

The case was brought to *trial*.

triangle ﹝'traɪˌæŋgl̩ ﹞ *n.* 三角形

He drew a *triangle* on the paper.

trick ﹝ trɪk ﹞ *n.* 把戲

I'm teaching my dog *tricks*.

trip ﹝ trɪp ﹞ *n.* 旅行

We went on a *trip* to Bali last week.

trouble ﹝'trʌbl̩ ﹞ *n.* 麻煩

It will be no *trouble* to drive you to the station.

trousers 〔'trauzəz 〕 *n.pl.* 褲子
(= *pants* 【美式用法】)
Please wear *trousers* for the trip tomorrow.

truck 〔 trʌk 〕 *n.* 卡車
They hired a *truck* to move their furniture.

true 〔 tru 〕 *adj.* 真正的
A *true* friend will always help you.

trumpet 〔'trʌmpɪt 〕 *n.* 小喇叭
My brother can play the *trumpet*.

trust 〔 trʌst 〕 *v.* 信任
I *trust* my parents in everything.

truth 〔 truθ 〕 *n.* 事實
Just tell me the *truth*.

try 〔 traɪ 〕 *v.* 嘗試
I'll *try* to learn French.

T-shirt 〔'ti,ʃɜt 〕 *n.* T恤 (= *tee-shirt*)
I love to wear *T-shirts*.

tub 〔 tʌb 〕 *n.* 浴缸
Jerry takes a cold bath in the *tub* every morning.

Tuesday (ˈtjuzdɪ) *n.* 星期二
(= *Tues.* = *Tue.*)
Tuesday is the day before Wednesday.

tummy (ˈtʌmɪ) *n.* 肚子 (= *stomach*)
My *tummy* hurts.

tunnel (ˈtʌnḷ) *n.* 隧道
Our car went through a long *tunnel*.

turkey (ˈtɜkɪ) *n.* 火雞
People often drink white wine with *turkey*.

turn (tɜn) *v.* 轉向
Go down the street and *turn* right.

turtle (ˈtɜtḷ) *n.* 烏龜
My younger brother has two *turtles*.

TV *n.* 電視 (= *television*)
Please turn on the *TV*.

twelfth (twɛlfθ) *adj.* 第十二的
December is the *twelfth* month.

twelve (twɛlv) *n.* 十二
One dozen equals *twelve*.

twentieth 〔'twɛntɪɪθ 〕 *adj.* 第二十的
Tomorrow will be the *twentieth* of March.

twenty 〔'twɛntɪ 〕 *adj.* 二十的
It took us *twenty* minutes to get to the station.

twice 〔 twaɪs 〕 *adv.* 兩次
I read the book *twice*.

two 〔 tu 〕 *adj.* 兩個
A bicycle has *two* wheels.

type 〔 taɪp 〕 *v.* 打字   *n.* 類型
Kate *types* well.
I don't like people of that *type*.

typhoon 〔 taɪ'fun 〕 *n.* 颱風
There were five *typhoons* this year.

U u

ugly 〔'ʌglɪ 〕 *adj.* 醜的
I think this painting is very *ugly*.

umbrella 〔 ʌm'brɛlə 〕 *n.* 雨傘
We use *umbrellas* when it rains.

uncle〔'ʌŋkl̩ 〕 *n.* 叔叔
Paul has only one *uncle*.

under 〔'ʌndɚ 〕 *prep.* 在…之下
A cat is sleeping *under* the tree.

underline 〔ˌʌndɚ'laɪn 〕 *v.* 在…劃底線
He *underlined* the sentence.

underpass 〔'ʌndɚˌpæs 〕 *n.* 地下道
Many people don't like to use *underpasses*.

understand 〔ˌʌndɚ'stænd 〕 *v.* 了解
Peter doesn't *understand* the words.

underwear 〔'ʌndɚˌwɛr 〕 *n.* 內衣
I prefer cotton *underwear* to linen.

unhappy 〔 ʌn'hæpɪ 〕 *adj.* 不快樂的
She is such an *unhappy* person.

uniform 〔'junəˌfɔrm 〕 *n.* 制服
Many students in Taiwan have to wear *uniforms*.

unique 〔 ju'nik 〕 *adj.* 獨特的
Everyone is *unique*.

unit (ˈjunɪt) *n.* 單位；單元

A gram is a *unit* of weight.

We finished *Unit* One this morning.

universe (ˈjunəˌvɝs) *n.* 宇宙

Are there other *universes* besides our own?

university (ˌjunəˈvɝsətɪ) *n.* 大學

Which *university* do you go to?

until (ənˈtɪl) *prep.* 直到 (= *till*)

She worked there *until* last month.

up (ʌp) *adv.* 往上

We must stand *up* when the teacher comes in.

upon (əˈpɑn) *prep.* 在…的上面

He laid a hand *upon* my shoulder.

upper (ˈʌpɚ) *adj.* 在上面的

He took down a book from an *upper* shelf.

upstairs (ˈʌpˈstɛrz) *adv.* 到樓上

Jessie ran *upstairs*.

us (ʌs) *pron.* we 的受格

They met *us* at the station.

U.S.A. ﹝ n. ﹞ 美國 (= *United States of America*)
My brother went to the *U.S.A.* to learn English.

use ﹝ juz ﹞ *v.* 使用
We *use* money to buy things.

used ﹝ just ﹞ *adj.* 習慣於…的 *v.* 以前
﹝ juzd ﹞ *adj.* 二手的
I am *used* to drinking a cup of coffee every
morning.
We *used to* play tennis every Sunday.
He bought a *used* car last week.

useful ﹝'jusfəl ﹞ *adj.* 有用的
A flashlight can be *useful* in the dark.

user ﹝'juzɚ ﹞ *n.* 使用者
The factory is one of the biggest *users* of oil
in the country.

usual ﹝'juʒʊəl ﹞ *adj.* 通常的
Staying up late is part of his *usual* routine.

usually ﹝'juʒʊəlɪ ﹞ *adv.* 通常
Mom *usually* leaves home at 6:30 in the
morning.

V v

vacation 〔ve'keʃən〕 *n.* 假期
They were on summer *vacation*.

Valentine's Day *n.* 情人節
Michelle got a lot of flowers on *Valentine's Day*.

valley 〔'vælɪ〕 *n.* 山谷
There is a river in the *valley*.

valuable 〔'væljəbḷ〕 *adj.* 珍貴的
He bought me a *valuable* ring as a birthday present.

value 〔'væljʊ〕 *n.* 價值
This painting is of great *value*.

VCR *n.* 錄影機 (= *video cassette recorder*)
Our *VCR* is out of order, so we want to buy a new one.

vegetable 〔'vɛdʒətəbḷ〕 *n.* 蔬菜
Rabbits mainly eat *vegetables*.

vendor (ˈvɛndɚ) *n.* 小販
Mr. Smith is a fruit *vendor*.

very (ˈvɛrɪ) *adv.* 非常地　*adj.* 正是；就是
The trees in the jungle are *very* tall.
That's the *very* thing I was looking for.

vest (vɛst) *n.* 背心
I need to buy new *vests*.

victory (ˈvɪktrɪ) *n.* 勝利
Our football team won a big *victory*.

video (ˈvɪdɪˌo) *n.* 錄影帶
Videos are not popular anymore.

view (vju) *n.* 風景；看法　*v.* 看
I like to see the *view* of the harbor.
What is your *view* on the subject?
A real estate agent came to *view* the house.

village (ˈvɪlɪdʒ) *n.* 村莊
There is a small *village* located on this island.

vinegar (ˈvɪnɪgɚ) *n.* 醋
You can use *vinegar* on salad.

violin 〔ˌvaɪə'lɪn〕 *n.* 小提琴
A *violin* is smaller than a viola.

visit 〔'vɪzɪt〕 *v.* 探望；參觀
We will *visit* my grandmother in Tainan.

visitor 〔'vɪzɪtɚ〕 *n.* 參觀者
The museum has many *visitors* every week.

vocabulary 〔 və'kæbjəˌlɛrɪ〕 *n.* 字彙
His *vocabulary* is large.

voice 〔 vɔɪs〕 *n.* 聲音
That man has a loud *voice*.

volleyball 〔'vɑlɪˌbɔl〕 *n.* 排球
Gina loves playing *volleyball*.

volume 〔'vɑljəm〕 *n.* 音量
He turned up the *volume* on the television.

vote 〔 vot〕 *v.* 投票 *n.* 票
People under 18 years old are not allowed to *vote* in an election.
If he gets a hundred thousand *votes*, he will win the election.

voter (ˈvotɚ) *n.* 投票者
This policy will not appeal to the *voters*.

W w

waist (west) *n.* 腰
Jane wears a belt around her *waist*.

wait (wet) *v.* 等待
Can you *wait* for me?

waiter (ˈwetɚ) *n.* 服務生
Alan's brother is a *waiter*.

waitress (ˈwetrɪs) *n.* 女服務生
The *waitresses* in this restaurant are very nice.

wake (wek) *v.* 醒來
Jane *wakes* up at 6:00 every morning.

walk (wɔk) *v.* 走路
You can *walk* to the store in five minutes.

walkman (ˈwɔkmən) *n.* 隨身聽
This is the latest *Walkman*.

wall ﹝ wɔl ﹞ *n.* 牆壁
The robber climbed over the *wall* to get away.

wallet ﹝'wɑlɪt ﹞ *n.* 皮夾
John carries his money in a *wallet*.

want ﹝ wɑnt ﹞ *v.* 想要
Anne *wants* a cold drink.

war ﹝ wɔr ﹞ *n.* 戰爭
Many people are killed in a *war*.

warm ﹝ wɔrm ﹞ *adj.* 溫暖的
Keep yourself *warm* in the winter.

was ﹝ wɑz ﹞ *v.* be 的過去式
Yesterday *was* my birthday.

wash ﹝ wɑʃ ﹞ *v.* 洗
We must *wash* our hands before eating meals.

waste ﹝ west ﹞ *v.* 浪費
Don't *waste* water.

watch (watʃ) *v.* 觀賞   *n.* 手錶

Mandy likes to *watch* cartoons before going to bed.

Mother bought a *watch* for me yesterday.

water ('wɔtɚ) *n.* 水

I want to drink a glass of cold *water*.

waterfall ('wɔtɚ,fɔl) *n.* 瀑布

The *waterfall* is beautiful to look at.

watermelon ('wɔtɚ,mɛlən) *n.* 西瓜

Watermelon is my favorite fruit.

wave (wev) *n.* 波浪

The *waves* are very high today.

way (we) *n.* 路

Can you tell me the *way* to the station?

we (wi) *pron.* 我們

We will go to the movies this weekend.

weak (wik) *adj.* 虛弱的

My grandfather is very *weak*.

weapon ('wɛpən) *n.* 武器

Are tears women's *weapon*?

wear (wɛr) *v.* 穿

She is *wearing* a new dress.

weather ('wɛðɚ) *n.* 天氣

The *weather* is good here.

wedding ('wɛdɪŋ) *n.* 婚禮

My parents' *wedding* was very romantic.

Wednesday ('wɛnzdɪ) *n.* 星期三

  (= *Wed.* = *Weds.*)

Wednesday is the day after Tuesday.

week (wik) *n.* 星期

There are seven days in a *week*.

weekly ('wiklɪ) *adj.* 每週的   *adv.* 每週地

  n. 週刊

They get a *weekly* pay.

We went to the beach *weekly*.

The *weekly* is very popular.

weekday ('wik,de) *n.* 平日

The museum is open on *weekdays* only.

weekend ('wik'ɛnd) *n.* 週末

What are you going to do this *weekend*?

weight (wet) *n.* 重量

Alex needs to gain some *weight*.

welcome ('wɛlkəm) *v.* 歡迎

We always *welcome* guests to our restaurant.

well (wɛl) *adv.* 很好地

She speaks English and Japanese *well*.

were (wɝ) *v.* be 的過去式

We *were* all tired out.

west (wɛst) *n.* 西方

The sun sets in the *west*.

western ('wɛstən) *adj.* 西方的

My house is in the *western* part of the town.

wet (wɛt) *adj.* 濕的

Be careful of the *wet* floor.

whale 〔 hwel 〕 *n.* 鯨魚

A *whale* is the biggest animal living in the sea.

what 〔 hwɑt 〕 *pron.* 什麼

I didn't know *what* you meant.

whatever 〔 hwɑt'ɛvɚ 〕 *pron.* 無論什麼
adj. 無論…的；任何…的

You can do *whatever* you want.

They will buy *whatever* books they like.

wheel 〔 hwil 〕 *n.* 輪子

Cars and buses move on *wheels*.

when 〔 hwɛn 〕 *adv.* 何時

When did John visit the zoo?

where 〔 hwɛr 〕 *adv.* 哪裡

Where do you live?

whether 〔'hwɛðɚ 〕 *conj.* 是否

I'm not sure *whether* it will rain.

which 〔 hwɪtʃ 〕 *pron.* 哪一個

Which of the two were you talking about?

while ﹝hwaɪl﹞ *conj.* 當⋯的時候 *n.* 一會兒

John came *while* I was washing the dishes.

I want to take a rest for a *while*.

white ﹝hwaɪt﹞ *adj.* 白色的

When people grow old, their hair turns *white*.

who ﹝hu﹞ *pron.* 誰

Who is the new boy in the class?

whom ﹝hum﹞ *pron.* 誰

（疑問代名詞或關係代名詞 who 的受格）

From *whom* is the letter?

The woman with *whom* I went is my aunt.

whose ﹝huz﹞ *adj.* 誰的

Whose shoes are those?

why ﹝hwaɪ﹞ *adv.* 為什麼

Why did she run away from home?

wide ﹝waɪd﹞ *adj.* 寬的

A *wide* road makes it easy for him to drive.

widen ﹝'waɪdn̩﹞ *v.* （使）變寬

Reading *widens* our knowledge.

The road *widened* there.

width〔wɪdθ〕*n.* 寬度
The bridge is 30 meters in *width*.

wife〔waɪf〕*n.* 妻子
His *wife* is a nurse.

wild〔waɪld〕*adj.* 野生的
We should protect *wild* animals.

will〔wɪl〕*aux.* 將
Cathy *will* play golf on Sunday.

willing〔'wɪlɪŋ〕*adj.* 願意的
I am *willing* to do the job.

win〔wɪn〕*v.* 贏
Rose will do anything to *win* the game.

wind〔wɪnd〕*n.* 風
The great *wind* blew across the sea.

window〔'wɪndo〕*n.* 窗戶
A car has four *windows*.

windy〔'wɪndɪ〕*adj.* 多風的
It's *windy* today.

wine ﹝ waɪn ﹞ *n.* 葡萄酒
She got drunk on one glass of *wine*.

wing ﹝ wɪŋ ﹞ *n.* 翅膀
I wish I had *wings* to fly.

winner ﹝ˈwɪnɚ﹞ *n.* 優勝者
Jack is the *winner* of the game.

winter ﹝ˈwɪntɚ﹞ *n.* 冬天
Winter is the season that comes after autumn.

wise ﹝ waɪz ﹞ *adj.* 有智慧的
My grandfather is a *wise* old man.

wish ﹝ wɪʃ ﹞ *v.* 希望
What do you *wish* to have for Christmas?

with ﹝ wɪθ ﹞ *prep.* 用
Peter writes *with* his left hand.

within ﹝ wɪðˈɪn ﹞ *prep.* 在…之內
You should finish the work *within* two days.

without ﹝ wɪðˈaut ﹞ *prep.* 沒有
We can't live *without* water.

wok 〔 wɑk 〕 *n.* 鍋子
My mother cooks with a *wok*.

wolf 〔 wʊlf 〕 *n.* 狼
Wolves kill sheep for food.

woman 〔 'wʊmən 〕 *n.* 女人
The *woman* with long hair is Tom's mother.

women's room *n.* 女廁
Could you tell me where the *women's room* is?

wonder 〔 'wʌndə 〕 *v.* 想知道   *n.* 奇蹟
I *wonder* why he didn't come.
It is a *wonder* that he survived the plane crash.

wonderful 〔 'wʌndəfəl 〕 *adj.* 很棒的
Ida and I had a *wonderful* time.

wood 〔 wʊd 〕 *n.* 木材
The chair is made of *wood*.

wooden 〔 'wʊdn̩ 〕 *adj.* 木製的
They bought a *wooden* house.

woods (wudz) *n.pl.* 森林
We went for a walk in the *woods*.

word (wɜd) *n.* 字
You can look up the new *words* in the
dictionary.

work (wɜk) *v.* 工作
Rebecca *works* in a bank.

workbook ('wɜk,buk) *n.* 作業簿
Our teacher asked us to complete three pages
in the *workbook*.

worker ('wɜkə) *n.* 工人
His father is a *worker*.

world (wɜld) *n.* 世界
Mt. Everest is the tallest mountain in the *world*.

worry ('wɜɪ) *v.* 擔心
Don't *worry* about me.

worth (wɜθ) *adj.* 值得… *n.* 價值
The book is *worth* reading.
The painting is of little *worth*.

would 〔wʊd〕 *aux.* will 的過去式
Would you like a cup of coffee?

wound 〔wund〕 *n.* 傷口
I have a knife *wound* on my arm.

wrist 〔rɪst〕 *n.* 手腕
John is wearing a beautiful watch on his
wrist.

write 〔raɪt〕 *v.* 寫
We *write* with pens or pencils.

writer 〔'raɪtɚ〕 *n.* 作家
A *writer* is someone who writes books.

wrong 〔rɔŋ〕 *adj.* 錯誤的
My answer was *wrong*, so I erased it.

Y y

yard 〔jɑrd〕 *n.* 院子
Children are playing hide-and-seek in the
front *yard*.

yeah 〔 jæ 〕 *adv.* 是的 (= *yes*)
Yeah, I see.

year 〔 jɪr 〕 *n.* 年
A new *year* begins on January 1st.

yearly 〔'jɪrlɪ 〕 *adj.* 一年一次的　*adv.* 每年地
I pay a *yearly* visit to my hometown.
We went abroad three times *yearly*.

yellow 〔'jɛlo 〕 *adj.* 黃色的
Shirley likes to wear her *yellow* dress.

yes 〔 jɛs 〕 *adv.* 是的 (= *yeah*)
"Is it raining?" "*Yes*, it is."

yesterday 〔'jɛstə·dɪ 〕 *n.* 昨天
It was raining *yesterday* but today the sky is
clear.

yet 〔 jɛt 〕 *adv.* 還 (沒)
The work is not *yet* finished.

you 〔 ju 〕 *pron.* 你
The teacher wants to see *you* for a moment.

young 〔 jʌŋ 〕 *adj.* 年輕的
Lucy is too *young* to have a baby.

your 〔 jʊr 〕 *adj.* you 的所有格
I'm glad to be *your* friend.

yours 〔 jʊrz 〕 *pron.* you 的所有代名詞
This book is *yours*.

yourself 〔 jʊr'sɛlf 〕 *pron.* you 的反身代名詞
Please take care of *yourself*.

yourselves 〔 jʊɚ'sɛlvz 〕 *pron.* you 的反身
代名詞
You are keeping *yourselves* busy.

youth 〔 juθ 〕 *n.* 年輕人
This club is for *youths*.

yucky 〔'jʌkɪ 〕 *adj.* 令人厭惡的
The school lunch is *yucky*.

yummy 〔'jʌmɪ 〕 *adj.* 好吃的
How *yummy* that cake was!

Z z

zebra (ˈzibrə) *n.* 斑馬

A *zebra* has black and white stripes all over its body.

zero (ˈzɪro) *n.* 零

The last digit of her telephone number is *zero*.

zoo (zu) *n.* 動物園

There are many kinds of animals in the *zoo*.

國中會考英語系列叢書

1.
   國中會考必備1200字【創新錄音版】
   劉 毅 主編 / 書 150元

   七、八年級同學可以先背「國中會考必備1200字」。按照字母順序排列，每一個單字皆有例句，讓同學對於單字的用法更清楚了解。

2.
   國中常用2000字【創新錄音版】
   劉 毅 主編 / 書附錄音QR碼 240元

   九年級同學可以進一步使用「國中常用2000字」，準備更完善。按字母序排列，每個單字皆有例句，讓同學更了解單字的用法。

3.
   國中分類記憶2000字【創新錄音版】
   劉 毅 主編 / 書附錄音QR碼 240元

   這2000字是教育部九年一貫課程綱要英文科小組參考多項資料後整理而得，也是國中英語教材編輯最重要的參考資料。

4.
   國中2000分類輕鬆背
   劉 毅 主編 / 書附錄音QR碼 250元

   將國中2000字分類，用「比較法」，利用已會的單字背較難的單字，化繁為簡，可以快速將單字背好，在最短的時間內，學最多的單字。

5.
   升高中關鍵500字
   劉 毅 主編 / 書 180元

   本書單字經過電腦統計，從無數的模擬試題中挑選出來編輯。每個單字均有例句，背單字同時訓練閱讀能力。

6.
   升高中常考成語
   謝沛叡 主編 / 書 100元

   包含歷屆基測、會考、高中職聯合入學測驗，各大規模考試英文試題中最常出現的關鍵成語。每個成語均有例句，附有「溫馨提示」，幫助學習。

7. 文法入門
劉 毅 修編 / 書 220元

學文法的第一本書，簡單易懂，一學就會。本書不僅
適合國中生，也適合高中生；適合小孩，也適合成人
；適合自修，也適合當教本。

8. 基礎英文法測驗
陳瑠琍 編著 / 書 100元

學英文靠自己，一天只花20～30分鐘，輕鬆學文法。
每課附學習成果評量，自我評估。附「重點」與「提
示」，複習容易誤用及難懂之處，澄清觀念。

9. 國中常考英文法
劉 毅 主編 / 題本 100元 / 教師手冊 100元

歸納出50個最重要的常考文法重點，每一個重點都有
10題練習題，讓同學在最短時間內把文法做完善的練
習和準備，並對文法有全面性的了解。

10. 會考單字文法500題
李冠勳 主編 / 題本 100元 / 教師手冊 100元

準備會考，一定要多做題目，本書共有50回單字文法
題，每一回10題，題型完全仿照會考，確實做完本書
，認真檢討答案，會考就能考高分。

11. 會考單字文法考前660題
李冠勳 主編 / 題本 150元 / 教師手冊 150元

本書共有66回單字文法題，每回10題，題型完全仿照
會考。做完本書所有題目，認真訂正答案，必能在會
考中勇奪高分。

12. 會考克漏字500題
李冠勳 主編 / 題本 100元 / 教師手冊 100元

針對會考克漏字題型編撰，「會考克漏字500題」有
70回，內容豐富，取材多元，為想加強克漏字的同學
量身打造。

13.
會考閱讀測驗500題
李冠勳 主編 / 題本 100元 / 教冊 100元

共有60回，內容廣泛，包含各種主題，是準備會考閱讀測驗不可或缺的閱讀題本。可以加強閱讀的速度和作答的準確度，更能從容面對會考閱讀測驗。

14.
會考聽力測驗500題
劉毅 主編 / 題本 100元 / 教冊附錄音QR碼 280元

收錄25回聽力測驗，每一回測驗完全仿照「會考」的題型出題。同學只要勤加練習，熟悉考試題型，訓練答題的速度，自然能在會考中取得高分。

15.
國中會考閱讀測驗①
李冠勳 主編 / 題本 100元 / 教師手冊 100元

收錄66回閱讀測驗，30回圖表判讀+30回文字閱讀，模擬最新會考閱讀測驗的兩種題型，輕鬆看懂圖表和文章，洞悉會考英文，一書雙贏。

16.
國中會考閱讀測驗進階①
李冠勳 主編 / 題本 100元 / 教師手冊 100元

新式會考閱讀測驗同時具有「圖表」和「文字」，相互參照作答。本書收錄35回閱讀測驗，內容生活化，圖文並茂，寓教於樂，為準備會考不可或缺的資料。

17. 國中會考英語模擬試題①②③④
劉毅 主編 / ①~④題本每冊 100元
①②教冊書+MP3、③④教冊附錄音QR碼 每冊280元

依照教育部公布「國中常用2000字」編輯而成。題型範例分兩部分：聽力、閱讀，各有8回，每回60題，由資深英語老師比照實際考試的方式出題，讓同學可以快速掌握出題方向，並做充足的準備。

18.

歷屆國中會考英語試題全集
劉毅 主編 / 書 220元

105年國中會考各科試題詳解
劉毅 主編 / 書 220元

106年國中會考各科試題詳解
劉毅 主編 / 書 220元

107年國中會考各科試題詳解
劉毅 主編 / 書 220元

108年國中會考各科試題詳解
劉毅 主編 / 書 220元

※鑑往知來，掌握會考最新趨勢。

19.

國中會考英語聽力入門
李冠勳 主編 / 書附錄音QR碼 280元 / 測驗本 50元

本書依照教育部公布之題型範例，分成三部分：辨識
句意、基本問答、言談理解，共18回，每回20題，適
合七、八年級同學提前練習會考聽力。

國中會考英語聽力測驗①②
劉毅 主編 / 每冊書附錄音QR碼 280元 / 每冊測驗本 50元

依照教育部公布之題型範例，分成三部分：辨識句意
、基本問答、言談理解，共12回，每回30題，題目豐
富，適合九年級同學，加強練習會考聽力。

國中會考英語聽力進階
劉毅 主編 / 書+MP3 280元 / 測驗本 100元

依照教育部公布之題型範例，分成三部分：辨識句意
、基本問答、言談理解，共15回，每回21題，題目豐
富，適合九年級同學加強練習會考聽力。

20.

國中生英語演講①②
劉毅 主編 / 每冊書+CD一片 280元

採用「一口氣英語演講」的方式，以三句一組，九句
為一段，共54回，以正常速度，三分鐘可以講完，如
果能夠背到一分半鐘內，就變成直覺，終生不會忘記
。書中內容可用於日常生活，也可用於作文中。

初級英檢公佈字彙【創新錄音版】
Key Words for Elementary
Level English Test

附錄音 QR 碼 售價：220 元

主　　　編 / 劉　毅
發 行 所 / 學習出版有限公司
　　　　　　TEL (02) 2704-5525
郵 撥 帳 號 / 05127272 學習出版社帳戶
登 記 證 / 局版台業 2179 號
印 刷 所 / 裕強彩色印刷有限公司
台 北 門 市 / 台北市許昌街 17 號 6F
　　　　　　TEL (02) 2331-4060
台灣總經銷 / 紅螞蟻圖書有限公司
　　　　　　TEL (02) 2795-3656
本公司網址 / www.learnbook.com.tw
電 子 郵 件 / learnbook0928@gmail.com

2024 年 3 月 1 日新修訂

ISBN 978-986-231-472-2